Away in a Manger

Also by Rhys Bowen

The Molly Murphy Mysteries

The Edge of Dreams
City of Darkness and Light
The Family Way
Hush Now, Don't You Cry
Bless the Bride
The Last Illusion
In a Gilded Cage

Tell Me, Pretty Maiden
In Dublin's Fair City
Oh Danny Boy
In Like Flynn
For the Love of Mike
Death of Riley
Murphy's Law

The Constable Evans Mysteries

Evanly Bodies
Evan Blessed
Evan's Gate
Evan Only Knows
Evans to Betsy

Evan Can Wait
Evan and Elle
Evanly Choirs
Evan Help Us
Evans Above

Away in a Manger

Rhys Bowen

 Minotaur Books ☀ New York

AWAY IN A MANGER. Copyright © 2015 by Rhys Bowen. All rights reserved. Printed in the United States of America. For information, address St. Martin's Press, 175 Fifth Avenue, New York, N.Y. 10010.

www.minotaurbooks.com

The Library of Congress Cataloging-in-Publication Data is available upon request.

ISBN 978-1-250-05203-2 (hardcover)
ISBN 978-1-4668-5336-2 (e-book)

Our books may be purchased in bulk for promotional, educational, or business use. Please contact your local bookseller or the Macmillan Corporate and Premium Sales Department at (800) 221-7945, extension 5442, or by e-mail at MacmillanSpecialMarkets@macmillan.com.

First Edition: November 2015

10 9 8 7 6 5 4 3 2 1

To my family, who make
the holidays so special

Away in a Manger

❧ One ☙

New York City, Wednesday, December 13, 1905

T is the Season to be jolly," sang the carolers outside Grace Church, while across Broadway the brass band of the Salvation Army thumped out "God Rest Ye Merry Gentlemen," in competition. It seemed as if the whole of New York City was suddenly caught up in the Christmas spirit. I maneuvered Liam's buggy along the crowded sidewalk, checking to make sure that Bridie was walking close beside me. In such a crowd one couldn't be too careful. Everyone seemed to be laden with packages and baskets of food items needed for holiday baking. It had been a year of optimism, with President Roosevelt elected for his first full term of office and the Wright brothers showing the world that airplanes really could stay up in the sky for more than a few seconds. We were definitely in the age of progress.

I pulled Bridie back from the edge of the street as an automobile drove past, sending up a spray of slush and mud. So much for the age of progress, I thought, as some of it

1

splashed onto my skirt. It had snowed the night before, the first snow of the season, creating an air of excitement, until the sun had come out and started to melt it, making the sidewalks slippery, dirty, and difficult to navigate. As we reached the corner of Tenth Street the young crossing sweepers were busy at work, clearing a pathway through the slush so that we ladies didn't get the hems of our skirts dirty.

"Merry Christmas. God bless you, lady," they called out, holding out raw little hands covered in chilblains. I felt guilty that I hadn't a penny or two ready for them, but the truth was that there were so many of them. How could I possibly choose one? And it was not only the crossing sweepers with their hands out. There were beggars of various sorts every few yards along Broadway, from hunched old women to pitiful children. Then there were those, like the crossing sweepers, one step up from beggars—the newsboys, the flower sellers with their tiny sprigs of mistletoe and holly. There were just too many of them. It hadn't been a year of progress for all of New York, that was clear enough. Immigrants were still arriving in their thousands, cramming into the already jam-packed Lower East Side and trying to support their families any way they could—many by selling a few eggs, roasted corn, bootlaces from a pushcart. I passed a baked potato stand with its enticing aroma. Several young boys stood around it, holding out their hands to the glowing charcoal until the owner drove them away.

As we moved away from the choir of carol singers, who were warmly wrapped in scarves and cloaks against the cold, I became aware of another voice—small, high, and beautiful.

"Away in a manger, no crib for a bed," it sang. "The little Lord Jesus laid down his sweet head."

Bridie heard it too and tugged at my sleeve. "Look, over there," she said.

I looked. A small girl was sitting in a doorway of Daniell's Haberdashery Store, huddled against the cold in a thin coat. She held out a tin cup as she sang, but people passed her without noticing her.

"Do you think she's an angel, come down for Christmas?" Bridie whispered to me.

She certainly looked like one. She had almost white-blonde hair and big blue eyes in a little heart-shaped face and her voice was so pure and sweet that it brought tears to my eyes.

"We have to give her something," Bridie said firmly, but I was already reaching into my purse.

"Go and give her that," I said, handing over a quarter.

She looked at it critically as if she thought it ought to be more, then took it and darted through the crowd to drop it in the girl's tin mug. The child looked up and gave Bridie an angelic smile. Her gaze fell on me and I had a strange feeling of connection.

Bridie made her way back to hang on to the buggy. "She looks so cold," she said. "Couldn't we give her some of my things? I know they'd be too big for her but at least they'd help her stay warm. Perhaps her mommy could make them into the right size for her."

I looked back. "She probably doesn't have a mommy," I said. "No mother would let her little child stay out begging in this weather. She's almost certainly an orphan."

"How sad," Bridie said. "To have nobody in the world to look after her. That's not fair."

"I'm afraid life isn't very fair," I said. I glanced back at the girl and saw that one of the crossing sweeper boys was now standing beside her. In all likelihood he'd take the money we'd just given her. It was very much a dog-eat-dog world in the lower levels of New York society. Then my gaze turned to Bridie, who had now blossomed into a sturdy eleven-year-old with the promise of becoming a beauty one day, and it occurred to me that she might well be an orphan herself now. I had brought her across the Atlantic from Ireland when her own mother was dying, and then Daniel's mother had taken her in when her father and brother had gone down to Panama to help dig the new canal. That had been a year ago, and we'd heard nothing from them since. And the news that had come from that hellhole had not been good—men dying like flies of yellow fever and other tropical diseases. So it might well be that we were all the family Bridie had in the world.

Of course she'd been well looked after by Daniel's mother, who had recently sent her to stay with me in the city, so that she could have a more normal education with girls her own age. It was also suggested that she could help me take care of Liam until I could find a proper hired girl to take the place of Aggie, who had died when our house was bombed. I would have taken Bridie in anyway, as I was now the closest thing she had to a mother, and I was glad when Daniel agreed to the arrangement. It was working very well. She was proving to be a willing little helper and good company.

"We'll look through your things and see what we can find for the little girl," I said. "And I'll buy you some yarn so that you can knit her a scarf. Mrs. Sullivan says you're a grand little knitter now."

Bridie beamed with pride. "I like knitting," she said. "And I like being here with you, taking care of Liam. I hope you don't find a new mother's helper too soon."

"I don't want you thinking that you're only here as my helper, Bridie," I said. "It's important that you get proper schooling, and my mother-in-law wants to turn you into a young lady."

She moved closer to my side. "But I like being with you best," she said. "You're the only mother I've got in the world."

I felt a lump come into my throat. There was nothing I'd like better than to keep her with me, but I knew that eventually Mrs. Sullivan would want to educate her and then introduce her into society better than I could. Daniel had also been urging me to find a properly trained servant to help me around the house and with Liam. I saw his point. In his position with the NYPD, status mattered. We should be entertaining more, and a husband who could not provide his wife with the luxury of a servant would be frowned upon. Nonetheless I was in no rush—having grown up in a cottage on the West Coast of Ireland, I was used to hard work and found it easy enough to keep our small house clean. And for all Daniel's urging, I could never see myself giving tea parties.

5

"The cattle are lowing, the baby awakes," I heard the sweet voice still singing. "But little Lord Jesus no crying he makes."

I turned to look back, puzzled. There was something about the song, or the way she was singing it, that didn't seem right, didn't fit. Something significant. Then I shook my head, not wanting to admit that Bridie had rattled me with her talk of angels. Where I came from in Ireland we were all too ready to believe in the miraculous. But this was New York and things that happened here were all too real.

We crossed Broadway, bumping the buggy over clumps of frozen mud and trolley lines, weaving between brewer's drays and cabs and watching out for more speeding automobiles. My son, Liam, slept on blissfully the way that only babies can, his long dark eyelashes brushing his cheek. I gazed at him now, thinking how chubby and healthy he looked, in contrast to that little . . .

"Do you think she really might be an angel?" Bridie asked suddenly. "Perhaps she's been sent down specially for Christmas to remind people to be good. We ought to give her more money. I've got two dollars saved up. She can have those."

I looked down at her tenderly. "I thought they were to buy Christmas presents with," I said.

"That girl needs the money more," she said. "I still have time to make Christmas gifts."

"You're a very kind person," I said, "but I'm afraid the world isn't quite as simple as you think. If we give the girl more money she probably won't be allowed to keep it. You saw that bigger boy. He's probably her minder and the money will end up with an even bigger boy or even an adult in charge of a gang. They put out pretty children to beg because they are more likely to touch people's heartstrings."

"That's terrible." Bridie was frowning. "That girl looks as if she never gets enough to eat. Let's at least make her a pie or something next time we come this way. No boy could take that away from her if she eats it quickly."

"We'll do that," I agreed, "and we'll see if you have any warm clothes that are too small for you now."

Bridie gave me a satisfied smile, then tugged at my sleeve again. "And one more thing."

"Yes?" I asked, expecting another charitable thought.

"Could we go and look at Macy's department store one day? They say their windows are all done up to look like magic."

"We can certainly do that," I said. "Liam might be old enough to enjoy seeing them too. So might I." And I grinned at her.

⚩ TWO ⚭

As soon as we got home Bridie rushed up to her room and took out all her clothes. Most of them had been made for her by my mother-in-law and were quite unsuitable for a beggar child—fine fabrics with lots of lace and embroidery. But we did come up with a woolen chemise and some woolen stockings. Bridie wanted to add a fine knitted shawl but I shook my head.

"Mrs. Sullivan will expect to see you wearing that when she comes for Christmas. She went to a lot of trouble to make that for you. It wouldn't be right to give it away. Besides, you might need it yourself if it gets any colder." I put my arm around her, noting that she was growing so fast she would soon be up to my shoulder. "We'll go to the dry goods store tomorrow and you can choose some yarn to knit her a scarf and mittens, all right?"

She nodded, smiling.

"Now we need to put all this away and get to work. Liam needs to be changed and fed, and I need to put Captain Sullivan's dinner in the oven."

I said the last with satisfaction. For once Daniel had no

major case keeping him out late at police headquarters. He had been able to eat dinner with us most evenings and even had some time to play with his son. I just prayed that nobody committed a murder or any other dastardly crime before Christmas, so that we could celebrate the holiday together.

I was particularly looking forward to Christmas this year. It would be the first one that Liam could actually enjoy with us, now that he was fifteen months and walking on his solid little legs. I pictured his excitement as he unwrapped a package with a toy inside. And we'd have a tree with glass ornaments and turkey and plum pudding. I sighed with contentment. We'd been through a lot this year. It was about time our life ran smoothly for a while.

I put a shepherd's pie in the oven, and was in the middle of feeding Liam his mashed carrots and milk pudding when the front door opened, sending a blast of icy air down the passage toward us.

"Papa's home," Daniel called. "Where's that boy of mine?"

Liam squealed in delight, squirmed, and tried to stand up in his high chair, luckily prevented by the straps. Daniel came into the kitchen, his cheeks bright red from the cold. "Brrr, it's chilly out there tonight," he said. "If it snows again it will stick this time. That wind off the Hudson cuts through like a knife. Don't tell my mother but I'm really glad for that scarf she knitted me."

He grinned as he came around the table to kiss me, then turned his attention to Liam.

"What's that you're eating?" he said. "Milk pudding? My favorite. I think I'll eat it all up." And he pretended to put his face down toward Liam's plate.

"No. Mine," Liam said clearly, making us both laugh.

"And how was your day, Miss Bridie?" Daniel asked as she brought a wet washcloth to clean up Liam's face.

"We met an angel," Bridie said. "At least she looked as if she could be an angel. She was singing very sweetly."

Daniel looked across at me and raised an eyebrow.

"We saw a beggar child on Broadway," I said. "She was singing 'Away in a Manger.' She really did have a sweet voice, poor little thing. We've looked for some of Bridie's outgrown clothes to give her, and Bridie's going to knit her a scarf."

Daniel frowned. "You want to be careful getting involved with people like that," he said.

"Daniel, she was a little child. She was shivering in the cold and singing."

"I'm sure she looked quite adorable," he said. "That's the whole point. We're having all sorts of trouble with pickpockets this season. More than usual. Anywhere there's a crowd. We suspect that one or more of the bigger gangs is involved. And a little child is exactly what the more sophisticated of the gangs would use."

"How could she pick pockets when she's sitting in a doorway?" I demanded, feeling my hackles rising now.

"She's the diversion, Molly. Don't you see?" he said patiently. "People hear her singing. They look across and see a sweet little girl and feel sorry for her. Some even put a penny or two in her cup. And while they are distracted a slick operator is taking their purse or going through their pockets."

"Oh, dear," I said. "I never thought of that. I suppose you may be right. How sad to use a child like that."

"She may even have a home and proper clothes when she's not working," Daniel said. "The beggar child in rags may be all part of the act."

I didn't want to think it but I realized it could well be true. There were plenty of slick criminals in New York City. Plenty of evil minds who would give no second thought to using a child for their schemes. But at that moment Bridie said angrily, "She wasn't a bad person. She wasn't. You could see it from her face. She looked like an angel. In fact I believe she is an angel, come down for Christmas."

Daniel ruffled her hair. "Perhaps she is," he said gently. "And she may well be a thoroughly nice child who has no choice about what she's being made to do. Anyway, let's talk of more cheerful things, shall we? I have the day off tomorrow—barring any major crimes overnight. So I thought we might take a trip uptown."

"Uptown?" I asked.

"I want to show Liam FAO Schwarz. You know," he went on when I looked puzzled, "the big fancy toy store on Fifth Avenue? I hear they have life-size toy soldiers outside and a fantastic train set running right across their windows."

"How lovely." I beamed at him. "And Bridie just asked today if we could visit Macy's store on Thirty-fourth. She's heard the windows there are all decorated for Christmas."

"We can do that too," Daniel said.

"But I have to go to school tomorrow," Bridie said. "We don't break up for Christmas until the day after tomorrow."

"I think they won't mind if you skip a day or so of school," Daniel said. "You've worked hard at your lessons. Besides, shopping uptown is educational." He winked at me. "And we need to buy a tree sometime soon. We'll need you to help choose."

"Oh, yes." Bridie's eyes lit up. "Can it be a big one? Will we put it in the front parlor window?"

"It can and we will," Daniel said. "Now I think we'd better take that young man out of his seat before he explodes with frustration."

He unstrapped Liam and threw him up in the air, making the boy squeal with delight again.

"Careful. He's just eaten," I warned. "It may come back all over you if you do that."

Daniel rapidly handed him back to me and I passed him to Bridie. "If you change him and put on his nightclothes he can come down and play with his daddy before dinner," I said.

As she went upstairs with the baby I turned to Daniel. "She has grown into such a helpful girl," I said. "She handles him so confidently. And he adores her."

"That's as maybe, but we still need a proper servant, Molly. You must see that," Daniel said. "You can't keep putting it off forever, just because of what happened. I know you have bad memories. But there are plenty of competent young women in New York City. And Bridie has to concentrate on her schooling and get an education with girls her own age. That was the understanding when my mother left her with us."

I nodded. "You're right. It's just that I like having her around. She's been like a daughter to me, Daniel."

"We can ask my mother to visit some of the agencies

with you when she arrives," Daniel said. "She's had experience in selecting reliable servants."

"I'm sure I can find a girl quite easily, Daniel," I replied stiffly. One thing I didn't want was a servant girl selected by Daniel's mother, who'd no doubt report back to the latter all my failings as a housewife and lady of society.

When I went up to kiss Liam good-night Bridie was sitting beside his cradle singing to him in her own soft and pretty voice. He was gazing at her, enraptured, and I paused in the doorway, not wanting to spoil the scene I was witnessing. Then Liam looked up and saw me, tried to scramble to his feet, encumbered by his long night-robes, and let out a wail.

"Oh, you terrible child. You were quite happy until you saw me," I said. "And Miss Bridie can sing you songs much better than I can."

I laid him down again firmly, stroking his head, and remembering, as I did almost every day of my life, how I had almost lost him.

"Go on singing," I said to Bridie. "You sing so prettily."

"That girl on the street," Bridie said thoughtfully. "Did you notice—she was singing 'Away in a Manger' with the same tune we sang it to in Ireland, not the way they sing it here."

So that's what had struck me as odd. In America they have a different melody for the Christmas carol from the one we learned in Ireland. Was it possible that the little girl was a newly arrived immigrant?

❊❅ Three ❅❊

T he next morning we awoke to find the world trans-
formed to white. Snow was still falling softly and
the cobblestones had vanished beneath a pristine
white blanket. I made pancakes with bacon for breakfast,
Daniel's favorite, and then I dressed us all warmly for the
trip uptown.

"Couldn't we just take those things over to the little girl
first?" Bridie asked.

"It's Captain Sullivan's one day off. We're going on an
outing today," I said. "We're going to see the store windows,
like you wanted. Aren't you excited?"

"Yes, but look how cold it is today. She'll be freezing."

I glanced across at Daniel. "All right. We can drop off
the clothes on our way and catch the trolley right there,"
I said.

"The trolley? I thought we'd take the El," Daniel said.

I shuddered. "I don't like traveling on the El ever
since . . ."

Ever since the accident, I said to myself. The accident when
the cars had plunged down from their rails and Liam and I

had narrowly escaped death in a car that remained hanging from the tracks.

"Molly, that won't happen again. And we'll take the Third Avenue line, not the Ninth."

"I know the trolley takes longer, but I'd still rather take it. And it goes right past Macy's," I said.

"All right. But you know it will be crowded. And cold."

"I like to be able to breathe the fresh air, rather than be shut up in a carriage with all those unsavory smells," I said.

"As you wish." Daniel sighed, knowing he was beaten. He took Liam from Bridie. "Come on, son. We're going on an adventure."

Bridie darted upstairs to get the package of clothing, then followed us out of the front door. Our footsteps crunched over snow and I held on to Daniel's arm as it was unsteady walking over hidden cobbles. The Salvation Army band was playing again as we came to Broadway. This time it was "See Amid the Winter's Snow," in an apt description of the scene we were witnessing. Snowflakes fluttered down around them, landing on their dark blue uniforms and settling on the peaks of their caps. Bridie was already peering ahead as I took her hand to cross Broadway.

"She's there. See. In that doorway," she called out excitedly, then broke away from me and darted through the crowd. The Salvation Army band was making such a din that I couldn't hear whether the little girl was singing or not, but she certainly looked up in surprise when Bridie dropped the package into her lap then sprinted back to us again without saying a word. I saw the child's puzzled, excited face as she began to undo the brown paper when we boarded our tram.

Macy's windows lived up to Bridie's expectations. She stared at each one, wide-eyed, her nose pressed against the glass until her breath steamed it over, hiding the scene inside. I have to confess if I hadn't experienced the shop windows in Paris earlier in the year I might have been equally impressed. There were mechanical rabbits eating carrots, figures skating on a frozen pond, an old toy maker sitting at his bench making toys. They were wonderful automatons, with the toy maker's eyes moving and his toys coming to life as he finished them.

Bridie would have stood there all day, I suspect. "Come on, my dear. We still have the toy shop to visit," I said.

She had just torn herself away reluctantly to join us when a strange thing happened. Daniel gave a shout. A skinny youth looked up and took off at great speed with Daniel hot on his heels. It was a mercy that Liam had just started fussing in Daniel's arms and he'd handed him over to me or I don't know what he would have done. If it had been an out-and-out running race I suspect that the boy would have gotten away, but he was hampered by the crowd dawdling along the sidewalk as they examined the windows, then a trolley coming to a halt made him change direction and slow enough for Daniel to grab him.

"Got ya, my boy," Daniel said, twisting his arm up behind his back.

"Let go of me," the boy shouted. "I ain't done nothing."

"If you haven't done anything, why were you running away?" Daniel demanded as the boy squirmed and fought.

"Wouldn't you run if a crazy lunatic started chasing you? Get your hands off me. I'll call the police."

"Oh, that's a good one. I am the police." Daniel almost looked as if he was enjoying himself. "Captain Sullivan. So I'm not only the police, I'm one of the most important policemen you're likely to meet."

"I ain't done nothing," the boy insisted. "Let go of me. You're hurting."

"I saw your hand going into that lady's bag," Daniel said.

"Go on then, search me!" the boy said belligerently. "You won't find nothing."

"Of course I won't. I stopped you in time. One more second and you'd have slipped her wallet under your jacket and been off through the crowd with her none the wiser."

"You can't prove that," the boy said. "And you'd better be careful, going around and accusing people of things they didn't do. There's such a thing as wrongful arrest, you know."

"Constable Macarthy!" Daniel boomed, and a stout man in uniform forced his way through the crowd toward them.

"A spot of trouble, Captain Sullivan, sir?"

"Do you recognize this young'un?" Daniel asked.

"Never seen him before, sir. What's he been doing?"

"Helping himself to people's wallets," Daniel said. "No, there's no point in searching him. I spotted him in the act of lifting a purse, but I suspect he's smart enough to have tucked others into hiding places to be retrieved later—just in case he was ever caught. Is that right, young fellow?"

"I said to get your hands off me," the boy snarled. "You're going to be sorry, you know. I got friends."

"Oh, no, I think it's you who's going to be sorry," Daniel said. "I never forget a face and my men will be on the look-out for you now, all over the city. If you're smart you'll stay indoors until after Christmas. Handcuff him, Constable."

"What do you want me to do with him, Captain?" the constable asked as the pair of them wrestled handcuffs onto the struggling and cursing youth.

"Take him to the nearest station house and get his name, address, and fingerprints," Daniel said. "If he gives you any sauce, you have my permission to lock him up for the night until he can learn some manners."

"You can't do that. I told ya, I ain't done nothing," the boy said, looking slightly more worried now.

"If you cooperate like a good boy, then you've got nothing to worry about and you'll be free as a bird in a little while," Daniel said. "But if any of my men catches you picking pockets again, remember we'll have your finger-prints on file and you'll be heading straight to jail. Under-stand me?"

A crowd had gathered, standing not too close but watch-ing with interest.

"What's the boy done?" a thin clergyman in a black suit asked.

"Pickpocket," Daniel said. "There are too many of them around this year. You should all make sure you keep a watchful eye on your cash."

"But he's only a boy," the clergyman said. "Surely hand-cuffs aren't necessary. If you'd let me have a word with him, I know I could make him—"

His speech was cut off by a scream from somewhere in

the crowd and a woman cried out, "My money is missing. Someone's taken my purse. Was that him too?"

"Either this one or one of his fellows," Daniel said. "Who's on this stretch of Broadway with you, Constable?"

"Dracott, sir. Over there on the corner of Thirty-fourth."

"Then you take the boy away and I'll send Dracott over to search likely hiding places to see if we can recover any more stolen wallets. We're probably too late. Undoubtedly this hooligan has a friend who's been following him to retrieve the stash. But from now on I want you to report to me every time there is a pickpocketing incident. This is prime territory over the holidays. You'll need backup."

"Thank you, sir. I'll take the boy now then, shall I?"

"Yes, and come right back. We'll need as many eyes as possible watching this crowd." He turned to the throng now surrounding him. "You can all help. Keep vigilant. Yell out if you see someone's pocket being picked. We need to put a stop to this right now." He moved within a few inches of the boy's face. "Don't forget. I'll be watching out for you. So will all my men."

The boy shot Daniel a look of pure venom as the constable marched him away. The crowd parted to let them through, then drifted away, back to their Christmas shopping. Daniel straightened his jacket and made his way back toward us. I didn't often have a chance to see him in action and again I marveled at his powerful presence, his calm demeanor. Then I remembered that every one of these encounters might put him in danger, every day of his life.

"It's just as I thought," Daniel said as he joined us and took Liam back from me. "This is something bigger than the usual opportunistic kid trying to take advantage of the holiday crowds. I'll wager he's part of an organized gang. Did you see the swagger? He wasn't even scared of me. He reckons he's got protection. And the constable hadn't seen him before. Our men usually know the potential trouble-makers on their own patch." He glanced back as the constable with the still struggling, cursing boy was swallowed up into the crowd. "I want to find out who's behind this and nip it in the bud. I want to know if they are recruiting boys off the street or if they are using known gang members. That's the problem—I can't assign extra men for what's essentially petty crime. But if it's one of the known gangs, I hate to see them extending their reach, and if it's a new gang, then I want to know about that too." Then he turned and gave me an encouraging smile. "Sorry about that. I'm supposed to have a day off, aren't I. Come on, let's enjoy ourselves. Toy store then a hot chocolate, I think."

I tried to feel as gay and carefree as before, but there was now a tension in the air that wouldn't quite go away.

❦ Four ❦

Is it far to the toy store?" Bridie asked. "My feet are cold."
"Too far to walk on a day like this," Daniel said. "We'll
take the Sixth Avenue El. Come on, there's a station
right over here."

He took my arm to steer me toward the elevated railway. I hesitated, still reluctant to travel after what had happened. But I told myself not to be silly. Just because one
train had plunged off the tracks once didn't mean it would
ever happen again. We crammed ourselves into a crowded
carriage and I was certainly glad when we reached Fifty-
eighth Street and I could breathe the fresh crisp air again.

Here uptown there was a different atmosphere. The
stores were swankier and almost every window was decorated with Christmas displays, electric lights, and even il-
luminated Christmas trees. Then we came at last to Fifth
Avenue and Daniel said, "There it is. FAO Schwarz. What
did I tell you?" He said it as if he was a conjurer who had
produced this for our pleasure.

There was a crowd around the store windows and at the
door two red-coated soldiers stood at attention as if this

was Buckingham Palace in London. Liam had been snuggled drowsily against Daniel's shoulder but perked up at the sound of Daniel's voice, and when he saw the real-life soldiers his eyes opened wide. We stepped inside and were greeted by a cacophony of sound. On one table a host of mechanical toys were moving around—bears turning somersaults, soldiers marching, drummers beating drums. And around the perimeter of the table a train set ran, hooting mournfully as it went over a bridge. Liam wriggled to get closer, staring wide-eyed.

"You're not quite old enough for that sort of thing yet," Daniel said, holding on to him. "But I can't wait for the day when I can get you a train set."

"We know who wants to play with the trains," I teased, and watched him grin.

"What should we get him for Christmas, do you think?"

"Don't discuss it in front of him," I said, giving Daniel a cautionary frown. "He has to think that it's coming from Father Christmas, or Santa Claus, or whatever you want to call him."

"He's one year old, Molly. He doesn't take in what we're talking about."

"I bet he does," I said. "We've a pretty smart child here, Daniel. Oh, look at the rocking horses."

"I've asked my mother to look out my old rocking horse," Daniel said. "It must still be up in the attic. I'll spruce it up for Liam."

"Not yet. He's too small for a rocking horse. Something he can push, maybe."

"How about a horse on wheels then?" Daniel asked. "I

had one of those when I was little, but I think it fell to pieces."

"That would be grand," I said, then I spotted the perfect thing. "Look, over there. The stuffed dog on wheels. Just the right size for him to push. Do you think it's very expensive?"

"It's Christmas, Molly. Hang the expense," Daniel said. "I'll come back and pick it up when he's not watching."

Bridie had been hanging back, not saying a word but gazing around her in awe. I noticed her expression and realized that in many ways she was still a child and hadn't had much of a childhood.

"Is there anything you'd want Santa Claus to bring you?" I asked.

She shrugged. "You already promised to buy me a skein of yarn to knit that girl a scarf," she said. "And I've outgrown my stockings."

"I don't think Santa Claus carries stockings on his sleigh," I said, smiling. I noticed she was looking wistfully at the china dolls. She was almost too old for dolls but had she ever had a proper one, with curls and clothes to dress her with? Daniel and his mother would think I was being silly, but I resolved to buy her a doll this Christmas.

"We'll get that wool for you this afternoon," I said. "I'm sure you want to start knitting right away."

She nodded, her face alight with excitement.

As we came around a big display of soldiers and forts we heard a shriek of laughter. What's more, I thought I recognized it. And sure enough there were my neighbors and dear friends Miss Goldfarb and Miss Walcott, usually known as Sid and Gus, standing together watching a mechanical bear. The bear turned somersaults then stood up again in a most realistic manner. As it flopped over in front of them they both burst into renewed and delighted laughter like a pair of children.

"So this is how you spend your days when you claim to be experiencing culture," I said.

"Where else should one be before Christmas?" Gus said. "What is more affirming of the beauty of life than the laughter of children?"

"I heard the laughter of two certain ladies," I said.

"Well, wouldn't you laugh?" Sid said. "Look at the face on this bear, Molly. He looks shocked and surprised every time he turns over." She wound the bear up again and put him down on the table where he started to turn somersaults in our direction. Liam took one look at him and burst into tears.

"Oh, dear," Gus said. "That's one toy we'll probably have to strike off our list. I suppose he is rather frightening for a one-year-old. But we've seen a fort and wooden soldiers. He has to have soldiers . . ."

"You're not to spoil him," I said. "One present is quite enough at his age. You've already been more than generous."

"But you know we love spoiling him," Sid said. "Even if we're not Catholic and not his official godmothers, we are self-styled fairy godmothers, aren't we, Gus?"

"Absolutely. So are you here to buy his Christmas presents?"

"Not while he's watching," I said. "We don't want to spoil the surprise." I glanced across at Daniel, who was holding Liam with a forced polite smile on his face. He didn't really approve of my friends and their bohemian lifestyle, however grateful he was for all they had done for me. And he certainly didn't approve of their dress, although today they were both wearing fur-trimmed capes and looked relatively civilized. It was only if one looked down that one could catch a glimpse of the trousers Sid often wore, and her short bobbed hair poked out from under a French beret she had acquired in Paris.

"So where are you off to now?" Gus asked. "You have to leave us alone to buy presents so they are a surprise to you too."

"Daniel's promised us hot chocolate before we go home," I said.

"You have to take the children to Central Park and let them play in the snow. Liam's first snow, Molly. On second thought, why don't we come with you? I'd love a good snowball fight, wouldn't you, Sid?"

"Rather!" Sid said. "And we can see if the lake is frozen."

Daniel opened his mouth to object then grinned and said, "Why not? We've nowhere else we have to be."

We crossed Fifth Avenue and went in through the park gates. Inside the park New Yorkers were already enjoying the first real snow of the season. Boys pulling younger siblings on sleds, children working together to make a snowman, snowball fights in progress. It made a colorful scene straight from a Christmas card. Daniel squatted down with

Liam and let him touch the snow. Liam reacted with shock and surprise then reached down to touch it again, scrunching it between his fingers and looking up at Daniel with a triumphant grin. I took him while Daniel helped the others make a small snowman, and then I watched while he and Bridie took on Sid and Gus in a snowball fight. They were having such a good time that I hated to interrupt them.

"Liam's getting cold," I said. "And as a matter of fact so am I."

Reluctantly the participants brushed the snow from their coats and gloves.

"Hot chocolate at the Viennese Bakery, I think," Sid said. "And pastries. Our treat."

Daniel didn't protest and we sat in the glorious warmth of the café, drinking hot chocolate with cream on top. I felt a great bubble of contentment inside. How rare it was that I had been able to enjoy a day of pure fun with my family and friends. This really was going to be a perfect Christmas—a reward for all that we had been through this year.

We caught the Sixth Avenue El home and Liam fell asleep against my shoulder. I nestled against the rough tweed of Daniel's coat, while Bridie stood at my knee. *Why had I ever resisted getting married?* I wondered. Being a family was the best feeling in the world.

❧ Five ❧

We stopped at Wanamaker's dry goods on the way home and Bridie chose bright red yarn. She started knitting as soon as she had taken off her coat. I didn't have the heart to interrupt her, and I took care of Liam and the dinner by myself.

"You know, I've been thinking," I said to Daniel as we sat at the table together after the meal. "You never want me to get involved in your work, and I appreciate that. But here's somewhere I could be useful to you. I'm an experienced detective. I've a good eye. I'm good at following without being observed."

Daniel was frowning, a wary look on his face.

I held up my hand. "Before you say anything, just hear me out," I said. "You say you can't spare men to catch pickpockets. I can keep my eyes open for you. I'm just another woman out doing her shopping and pushing a buggy."

"What would be the point, since you couldn't chase after anyone or arrest them?"

"I'm trying to be helpful, Daniel. You've said yourself I'm a good detective. I am. If I see pickpocketing going on I'll take down an accurate description and hand it to the nearest constable. What could be wrong with that?"

"Nothing, I suppose," Daniel said hesitantly. "As long as you didn't do anything foolish like trying to apprehend anyone."

"Can you see me trying to wrestle a great lad the way you did?" I demanded. "Of course I wouldn't be that silly, especially if I had Liam and Bridie with me. But you yourself said you'd like to find out if these were newly recruited boys or known gang members. If I can provide you with some good descriptions you may be able to put a name to a face."

I could see him weighing this. One part of him didn't want his wife involved in anything vaguely criminal and dangerous, but he had to admit that I could indeed be useful.

"And I've had another thought," I said. "I could even set myself up as bait—put a nice empty purse in the top of my shopping bag—maybe attached to the bag with a string, so that when they try to take it . . ."

"Oh, no," Daniel said. "That's going too far."

"I don't see why," I said. "If I feel the purse being jerked I can scream, 'Help. Pickpockets, thieves. He tried to take my purse!' And he'll run away and at least other people on the street will be alerted and saved from being robbed."

"And if he knocks you down in anger and frustration? If he snatches Liam out of the pram?"

"He wouldn't. Liam is firmly strapped in, as you know."

"If he notices who you are and tells his boss and they

come by later to retaliate? We are dealing with the under-world, you know. They have no scruples."

That, of course, struck home. A gang had already tried to kill us once this year. They had blown up our house and killed our little servant girl as she tried to protect Liam. There was no way I'd want to risk Liam's life again.

I nodded. "I do see your point and you're right. I'll stick to being the unobserved observer then. Although I'd dearly love to catch one of them red-handed. How can these people have no conscience, stealing hard-earned cash like that? I suppose I could understand if anyone wanted to rob the rich. But everyone around here is a recent immigrant, working hard to earn an honest penny."

"Criminals have no conscience," Daniel said. "Surely you've learned that by now. If you or I help ourselves to the cookie jar when we're told no cookies before dinner, we'd feel guilty and not enjoy the cookie. A criminal doesn't think that way. His only concern is whether he'll be caught or not. If he's not caught, he feels clever because he's cheated society."

"How horrible." I shuddered. "Do you think they are born that way or that society makes them like that?"

"I've no idea," Daniel said. "Ask your friends across the street. They've been studying psychology with Professor Freud, haven't they? I'm sure they'd tell you that criminals take it out on society because they felt rejected by their mothers or other such twaddle."

I smiled. "My mother was never particularly nice to me. In fact I could never do anything that was good enough for her. But that made me more determined to be a good mother to my own children."

Daniel reached across and squeezed my hand. "And you are. I feel so lucky to have you and Liam, and hopefully many more to come. It's going to be a grand Christmas this year, isn't it?"

I was about to turn out the lamps when I spotted Bridie, still sitting in a corner, knitting furiously. The scarf was at least a foot long.

"Time for bed," I said. "You'll strain your eyes if you sit up any longer."

"But I really want to finish this and give it to the girl," she said.

I shook my head and steered her up the stairs. "One more day won't make much difference to her, and she already has your warm underclothes," I said.

But when I came down in the morning Bridie was already sitting at the kitchen table, knitting away. The scarf was a good deal longer.

"When did you get up?" I asked.

"A while ago. I wanted to get this finished today whatever happens."

"It's looking lovely," I said. "You can be really proud of your work. After you've finished we'll buy some more yarn and you can knit Mrs. Sullivan a similar scarf for a Christmas present. She'll be arriving in a couple of days."

As I said these words my heart lurched. My mother-in-law would indeed be arriving early next week, which meant the whole house would have to be cleaned, sheets ironed, and everything looking just perfect. Maybe I'd do what

Daniel had been urging, go out and hire a servant right away. But in truth I was in no hurry for that to happen. Between Bridie and myself, we could keep the place running quite smoothly, and I wasn't sure I would enjoy having a stranger under my roof. Maybe when another child came along, I'd think about it again.

I was anxious to be out on the streets in the hunt for pickpockets, but Bridie was knitting away furiously and there was the housecleaning to do. In case you think I run a messy establishment, I do not. I like to think my house is clean and neat most of the time, but Daniel's mother would be bound to find the one corner I hadn't dusted. So while Bridie knitted I went over the front parlor, laying the fire ready to be lit when we had company and taking the rug outside to be beaten. I came in with my cheeks and hands burning from the cold.

Bridie scarcely stopped to eat, and the scarf was finished when the ball of yarn ran out about three o'clock. I helped her put tassels on both ends, then we found some tissue paper and wrapped it up and set off to find the little girl. I wondered if she might have gone home, as the light was fading fast and it was cold and damp. But there she was, hugging her knees to herself in her doorway, not even trying to sing. Bridie hung back, suddenly shy.

"Go on," I urged, pushing her forward. "It's your present. Go and give it to her. Tell her it's an early Christmas gift."

Bridie went shyly up to the child and I watched her face light up with recognition.

"Thank you very much for the stockings and the vest," she said. "They are lovely and warm."

"This is an early Christmas present," Bridie said, and handed it to her.

"A present? For me?"

"I made it for you," Bridie said.

Slowly she opened it and looked up with wonder. "It's beautiful." And she wrapped it around her neck. "You are very kind."

"What's going on?" The crossing sweeper boy I'd seen before pushed through the crowd to us.

I remembered what Daniel had said about the gangs using children and a bigger child always acting as their minder to take things away from them. I took a step forward, ready to intervene, but the little girl was showing off the scarf, her face still alight with joy.

"Look, Tig. She made me a scarf."

"Why did you do that?" he asked, his face still defiant. "You don't know her."

"Because she was cold," Bridie said, staring back with equal defiance. She was slightly taller than he, and a good year or two older. "I heard her singing. It was lovely."

"It was very kind of you," he muttered, now clearly embarrassed by Bridie's presence. "We appreciate it. Thank you on behalf on my sister."

Then he gave a little half bow and pushed his way back through the crowd to his crossing, carrying his broom. So he was the child's brother. I stared after him, frowning.

"Good-bye." Bridie waved to the little girl. "I have to go now. I hope you enjoy your scarf." And she ran back to my side.

We went on our way, saying nothing. Bridie, I suspect,

was still in the glow of what she had done. I was trying to make sense of what I had just seen and heard. I knew what street children sounded like. "I ain't done nothing," the boy Daniel had arrested had said. And yet this boy spoke like an educated person, older than his years, and with what sounded almost like an English accent. And hadn't the little girl used the word "vest" instead of "undershirt"? What in God's name were two upper-class English children doing on the streets of New York?

❧ Six ❧

S o did you give your present to the beggar child?"
Daniel asked when he came home that night.

Bridie nodded, glancing up at him shyly and
going pink. She was always tongue-tied in his presence.
"And she said that it was beautiful and I was very kind."

"She did," I agreed, coming from the stove with the
Irish stew and placing it on a mat in the middle of the table.
"She and her brother were both very well-spoken, and
they sounded as if they could be English too. How can
that be?"

Daniel shrugged. "All sorts of people come here as immigrants. There are Jewish professors playing the violin on
the streets in the hope of pennies. It's not easy to start a
new life here, as we know. And if their parents died or were
taken ill, maybe they suddenly found themselves with nobody to take care of them. That's what happens when you
move far from home and family, isn't it?"

"That's awful. We should do something."

Daniel reached out and patted my hand. "Molly, New
York is full of beggar children. There's nothing you can do

to change things except knit a scarf like Bridie here. Thanks to her, one little girl will be a bit warmer tomorrow."

Bridie beamed as she started to ladle Irish stew onto the plates.

After the meal, when Bridie volunteered to wash up for me, Daniel and I took a cup of tea through to the back parlor—a luxury that didn't happen often in the life of a policeman.

"You know what I suggested about keeping an eye open for pickpockets?" I said, stirring sugar into my cup.

"You're not telling me you've spotted one already?"

"No, we were only on Broadway for a minute," I said. "Bridie became suddenly shy when the boy thanked her profusely and she couldn't wait to be away. But I was thinking about those children—they are there, on that street, all day, every day. I'm sure the little girl is sharp-eyed and she has nothing to do except watch people. Perhaps they could watch out for pickpockets and we could give them a small reward when they report seeing one."

Daniel frowned. "How old would you say that child is? Four or five maybe? How could one rely on the word of a four-year-old? And how do you think she'd be treated if it was found out that she'd snitched on a fellow street urchin? Beaten up at the very least. Perhaps even killed if a gang is involved. I don't think you'd want to risk her life, would you?"

"Of course not," I said. "I was just trying to think of a way to give them some extra money while helping you."

He smiled. "You've a good heart, Molly Murphy. I'll say that for you."

"But you wouldn't object if I slipped her the odd coin when I went past?"

"By all means. But do realize that it's all too possible it will be taken from her by the kingpin of the block and you'll be funding petty criminals. Bridie's outgrown clothing is more practical and safer."

"All right." I sighed. Why did the world have to be so complicated?

The next day I really wanted to be out on the streets, keeping an eye out for pickpockets. I think secretly I wanted to prove to Daniel how useful I could be to him if he'd only include me in more of his cases. But alas, it was a fine bright day, and I had to take advantage of that and get laundry done and hung out on the line to dry. Fine days could not be counted on at this time of year and the diapers piled up rain or shine. Then it was ironing sheets to put on Mrs. Sullivan's bed and giving her bedroom a good clean and polish. She'd be sure to notice if there was dust under the bed.

I don't know why I was still so intimidated by my mother-in-law, but I was. And I'm not usually the sort of person who lets herself be bullied or cowed either. Maybe it was because she'd made it so clear from the start that she was disappointed in Daniel's choice of a bride. She and her husband had had high hopes for him, sending him to Columbia University, seeing him mixing with the highest levels of society who would help him move into politics one day. They'd been delighted when he'd become engaged to a society beauty—and then instead he'd married little Molly Murphy, newly arrived from an Irish peasant's cottage.

She'd never said anything outright, but she could never

resist telling Daniel when the children of her friends and neighbors made good matches and linked themselves to the Roosevelts or Vanderbilts or other families that mattered. Daniel seemed quite unimpressed by this and even made amused comments, for which I was grateful. But I always felt those watchful eyes on me as I went about my tasks, and read the unspoken thought: *She's not good enough for my son.*

She'd been civil enough to me, even solicitous when I was expecting Liam, but I'd never quite warmed to her. Maybe it had something to do with my own mother always finding fault. Nothing I did was ever good enough for her. Maybe I saw my mother-in-law as a reincarnation. Maybe her remarks were meant to be innocent. But then again, maybe not.

After Liam had awoken from his afternoon nap and a big pile of clean diapers lay folded on his shelf, I decided that we really could take a walk.

"Do you want to see your little friend wearing her scarf?" I asked Bridie.

"Oh, yes, please." She bounded to get her overcoat and hat.

The bright morning had given way to heavy clouds with the promise of more snow, and the wind, channeled between tall buildings, was bitter. I turned up my coat collar and tucked Liam's blankets more firmly around him. The snow had partially frozen and been pressed by carriage wheels into ruts, making pushing the buggy hard work and bumpy for Liam—who didn't seem to mind but sat up, peering out excitedly.

We turned onto Sixth Avenue and immediately I became vigilant, watching the students coming from the university and the housewives returning with the ingredients for their evening meals. But I didn't expect to find the pickpockets working here. These really were the poor people, hardly worth stealing from. It was on Broadway with Wanamaker's and the other big dry goods stores, and the carol singers, that people would be caught up in the excitement of the season and let down their normal guard.

We followed Eighth Street then turned northward on Broadway, Wanamaker's taking up the whole block on the east side, and today a group of handbell ringers stood outside the main entrance ringing out "We Wish You a Merry Christmas." The sweet sound of the bells echoed through the cold air and the smell of roasting chestnuts greeted us from a barrow being pushed slowly along the edge of the street. I stood under the awning of Wanamaker's doorway, purporting to be listening to the handbell ringers but in reality watching the crowd as they came in and out of the store.

"Come on, Molly." Bridie tugged at my sleeve. "It's too cold to stand still today and I want to see my girl and her scarf."

I decided that having a lively eleven-year-old and a baby with me would not make for easy detective work. When Mrs. Sullivan arrived maybe I could slip out alone and do some proper observation. I made Bridie hang on to the buggy as the policeman blew his whistle for us to cross the street. It was slushy and muddy and we slithered our way across. I wished a crossing sweeper had been operating here, but there was too much traffic and it never stopped. The crossing sweepers were working hard, however, when we crossed Tenth, and a narrow ribbon of street was quite free of mud and snow. The well-spoken big brother was among the sweepers and gave me a half smile. I reached into my pocket and pulled out the silver dollar I had put there. "This is for you and your sister," I said. "It's probably safer to give it to you, so that it won't get taken away from her."

His eyes opened wide as he looked at the coin in his hand. "Thank you very much, ma'am," he said. "You are very generous."

"Make sure your sister gets a warm meal," I said.

"I will. I will." He nodded then rushed back to sweep as a loaded dray spattered mud over the street.

Bridie was tugging impatiently as we continued to the doorway where the little girl sat. We heard her voice before we saw her. "In the bleak midwinter, frosty wind made moan," she sang in that beautiful angel voice. And there she was, hugging her knees to her for warmth, and . . .

"Where's your scarf?" Bridie demanded. "Why aren't you wearing your scarf?"

The child stared up at Bridie with big, sad eyes. "She took it away from me," she said, her voice trembling.

"Who did?" I demanded angrily.

"Aunt Hettie. She didn't believe it was mine. She said I must have stolen it."

"Your aunt thought you'd stolen it?" I said.

She nodded, biting back tears now. "I told her a lady and

a girl had given it to me but she wouldn't believe me. Then she said it was too good for me and she took it away. Tig said that she's probably going to sell it."

"You live with your aunt?" I asked, having taken them for street children with their obvious lack of care and threadbare clothing.

She nodded. "Aunt Hettie."

"Then I'm going to have a word with this Aunt Hettie of yours," I said. "I'll let her know that we made the scarf for you and she should be ashamed of herself sending you out into the cold dressed the way you are."

"Oh, please don't," she said, reaching out to grab at my skirt. "She doesn't like us very much. She might turn us out and then we'd have nowhere to go."

At that moment a woman's voice screamed out, "My purse! Someone just took my purse!"

❧ Seven ❧

The constable on the corner sprang into action. He blew his whistle as he hurried over to the woman.

"It was here a second ago," the woman shouted. "I know because I checked when I was standing on the street corner, waiting to cross. They said you couldn't be too careful around Christmastime."

"Anyone see anything?" A crowd started to gather. The constable looked through the crowd and his gaze fastened on a skinny youth, leaning against the wall with his hands in his pockets. "You," he said. "You look like you might be up to no good."

"Me? I'm just standing here minding my own business and waiting for my pal to show up," the boy said. "But come to think of it, I did see something. That kid over there. I saw him standing real close to that lady and I think he took something out of her bag."

And to my horror he pointed out our little girl's brother.

"Right, my boy. You're coming with me." The constable took a couple of big strides and grabbed him by the collar before he could move.

"Let go of me. I didn't steal anything," the boy cried out, struggling as the constable held him fast.

"Then let's look through your pockets, shall we?" the constable said. He reached into the boy's jacket and held up something in triumph.

"And what's this, then? How does a boy like you come by a whole dollar? A nice shiny silver dollar? Not the sort of change you get from sweeping the street, is it?"

"A lady gave it to me," I heard him say as I tried to force my way through the crowd. "She said it was for me and my little sister."

The little girl was on her feet now, grabbing at me frantically. "Don't let him take my brother away," she begged. "He's a good boy. He doesn't steal."

I was going through a turmoil of indecision. I remembered all too clearly Daniel's warning that some street children might look sweet and innocent, but it was just a guise to prey on passersby. What if he was a pickpocket and his little sister didn't know or didn't realize?

But my gut instinct won out. Any child who had thanked us so gratefully for our small gifts surely couldn't be a thief.

"Hold on to Liam's buggy," I instructed Bridie. "Watch over him carefully and I'll be right back."

Then I forced my way between two large Italian ladies and their shopping baskets.

"Hold on a minute, Constable," I called. "I gave that boy the dollar."

The crowd turned to face me.

"You did, ma'am?"

"A few minutes ago. My little girl has been most concerned about this boy's small sister, who sits in that doorway down there, begging. So I thought I'd help them out
with a dollar."

"Most generous of you, ma'am," he said. Then he
frowned at me. "Wait a minute, I know you, don't I? It's
Mrs. Sullivan, the captain's wife, isn't it?"

"That's right."

"Well, Mrs. Sullivan, ma'am. I'm afraid this young rascal
could well have taken your dollar, all innocent-like, and
then helped himself to another lady's purse the next instant.
We see it all the time. Rogues and ruffians, the lot of them."

"I think this boy is different, Constable," I said. "I don't
think he stole any purse."

"I didn't," the boy said, his eyes pleading with me. "I've
never stolen anything in my life—apart from some extra
potatoes from Aunt Hettie."

The constable was looking first at the boy and then at
me. "If you're vouching for the boy, Mrs. Sullivan, then I
have to believe he's okay. But a lot of the little rascals around
here would sell their own grandmother for a nickel." He
continued searching the boy as he spoke. "There doesn't
seem to be a purse on him, but I've been instructed to take
suspected pickpockets down to the station house and
have them fingerprinted."

"If I vouch for him, then I hope that won't be necessary,"
I said. "I tell you what—I'll take the boy home right now
and have a word with his aunt. You can see he doesn't have
the purse on him, can't you? Let's assume he's innocent. In

fact I'm rather inclined to believe that the boy who identi-fied him was the real thief himself, or was in league with him."

We both looked around and, as I suspected, the bigger boy had vanished.

"He wanted time to get away," I said.

The constable was frowning now, torn between doing his instructed duty and wanting to believe me.

"He did have a shifty sort of look about him," he said. "What's more I think I've seen him hanging around here before."

"There you are, then," I said. "I'll take this young man straight to his aunt's house and we'll have a little talk. We'll make sure that nothing like this happens again, all right?"

The constable released the boy. "If you say so, Mrs. Sul-livan." He turned to the boy and wagged a finger at him. "Now you be grateful to this lady, you hear me? If it wasn't for her you'd be spending the night at the station house jail, along with thugs and murderers. And if you really took that purse, then I'll be watching out for you next time. I'll have my beady eye on you from now on."

"I really didn't take it, Officer," he said. "I promise. My mother brought us up properly."

The constable grinned as he looked at me. "Hark at him talking. He sounds like a proper Little Lord Fauntleroy, don't he? Where did you get such posh ways, my boy?"

"From my mother," he said.

"And where's your ma now?"

"She's gone." The boy's face became a blank mask.

I put an arm around his shoulder. "Come on. I've promised to take you home and your sister is waiting with my children."

Tig bent to snatch up his precious broom, then allowed me to usher him away. The crowd parted for us, as if we were bewitched. I think they'd heard the boy speak too and were looking at him with wonder and suspicion. The little girl rushed up to her brother and flung her arms around him.

"You're safe, Tig. They said you were going to prison."

He hugged her fiercely. "It's all right, Emmy. This lady saved me. The constable was going to arrest me but she told him that she'd vouch for me."

Emmy looked up at me, eyes glowing. "Are you really our fairy godmother?" she asked.

I smiled. "You can blame Bridie here. She was the one who heard you singing and wanted to do something for you. She sat up almost all night knitting that scarf for you. The one your aunt took from you. No matter. We'll soon sort that out. Come on. Where do you live?"

The children looked at each other with frightened faces. "A long way from here," the boy, Tig, said. "Look, you don't really have to speak to our aunt, do you? If she thinks I've been stealing that will be a good excuse to get rid of us. She's always threatening to."

"She doesn't sound like a very nice person," Bridie said as we set off down Broadway, heading south. "And she steals scarves too."

"She's absolutely horrible," Emmy said. "We hate her. But we've nowhere else to go. Mummy left us with her so we have to stay, until she comes back."

45

"How long has your mother been gone?" I asked.

Emmy frowned. "A long while," she said. "She went away soon after we came to America."

"Where did you come from?" I tried not to sound too curious.

"England," Emmy said, confirming what I had surmised. "We came from England. That's where we used to live. And then we went to stay with Aunt Hettie when we got here."

"And when do you expect your mother back?"

"We don't know," Emmy said. "We just keep waiting and waiting but she doesn't come and she doesn't even write to us."

"You don't know where she's gone? Didn't she say where she was going?" I asked. This time I heard the anxiety in my voice.

"She didn't tell us, but she promised she'd be back soon and that everything would be all right again if we were good and did what Aunt Hettie told us."

"Emmy, I don't think you should be telling this lady everything like this," Tig interrupted sharply. "She's been very kind, but she's a stranger. Remember what Mummy said about being careful in a strange city, and how dangerous it was here. We shouldn't tell a stranger things. For all we know she's a child snatcher."

Emmy looked up, suddenly frightened. "You're not a child snatcher, are you?"

I laughed. "I promise you I'm not. As you can see, I've a baby of my own and a visiting eleven-year-old to take care of, as well as a husband. I don't need more children to snatch. And my husband is an important man in the New York police, by the way."

"Oh, he's a police captain," Tig said, letting down his guard again. "When that constable called him captain I thought he was on a ship."

"So where are we going?" I asked. "Where does your aunt live?"

"Over on West Street by the waterfront," Tig said. "It's quite a long way, and it's starting to snow again. Do you really have to come with us?"

"I promised the constable I'd take you home," I said. "Besides, I'd like to see this aunt of yours for myself. I won't mention the pickpocketing, if you like. I really don't think you took that lady's purse."

"I didn't," he said indignantly. "We were brought up properly. Mummy and Daddy were very keen on manners and doing everything correctly."

"What happened to your father?" I asked. "He didn't come over to America with you?"

"He died," Emmy said. "He died a long time ago."

"It was two years ago," Tig corrected. "It seems like a long time to you because you're only four. It's half your life."

"I'm almost five." She stuck out her little chin. "You said I'd be five right after Christmas."

"And how old are you, Tig?" I asked. "What is Tig short for? It's not a name I've heard."

"I'm eight years old," the boy said, "and my real name is Thomas, after my father. Thomas Jones."

"That sounds like a Welsh name," I said.

"My father was from Wales," he agreed.

"Ah, so that's why your sister has such a lovely singing voice." I looked down at Emmy and smiled. "The Welsh are reputed to be fine singers. It's in the blood."

"Our father was a wonderful singer," Tig agreed, and for the first time I saw the ghost of a smile cross that tense and worried face. "He sang in front of people. On a stage."

"My mummy is a beautiful singer too," Emmy said. "She has a lovely voice and we used to sing with her. It made her feel happy after Daddy died, didn't it, Tig."

"Uh-huh," Tig agreed. I sensed that the subject was painful for him.

"So is your name short for Emily?" I asked Emmy.

"No, it's really Megan," Tig said for her. "Mummy's name is Margaret and Megan is the Welsh way of saying it."

"Did you live in Wales? Do you speak Welsh?"

Tig shook his head. "Daddy could speak Welsh. He taught us some Welsh songs. But we never lived there. We lived in London." He glanced up at me as we stood ready to cross the road. "Do you really have to speak to Aunt Hettie? I don't want to make her cross with us."

"You don't really think your aunt would turn you out, do you?" I asked. I steered my little brood through the traffic and we turned onto Waverly Place, in the direction of the Hudson.

"She said she would the other day. She never thought our mother would be gone so long, you see, and she says she can't afford to feed us."

"That's why you sweep and sing?"

He nodded, then walked on ahead, clearly uncomfortable at talking to me.

"She says she doesn't want us about the house getting under her feet in the daytime." Emmy was more ready to tattle on the hated aunt.

"And you have no other relatives you could go to? Doesn't your aunt know where your mother has gone?"

"I don't know," Tig said bleakly. "Nobody tells us anything."

And I realized that they were little children. Children accept where they are being taken. If Mummy says, "Goodbye and I'll be back soon," they trust her. They don't cross-question where she's going or when she will return. But surely she would have told the aunt when she asked her to take care of the children. Surely the aunt would have tried to contact someone when the mother didn't return. While my head was telling me that this was none of my business, my heart was whispering, *You are a detective. You could find out what happened to their mother and why she left them with such an unsuitable aunt in a strange city.* Something about their story certainly didn't make sense. They had precise, upper-class accents but an aunt who sent them out begging. A thought occurred to me. "Tig, it was definitely your mother, your own mother, who brought you from England to America?"

"What do you mean?" He turned back to me, confused.

"I just wondered if . . ." I shook my head. "Never mind. It doesn't matter."

We walked on, our footsteps crunching on hardened snow. Then Tig blurted out, "Pardon me and I'm not being rude"—he stood his ground, facing me now—"but you are asking an awful lot of questions and Mummy said it wasn't polite to be too inquisitive."

"I just want to help you, Tig," I said. "You are obviously not being very well looked after by your aunt, and I wanted to know if I could do anything to help."

"You can't," he said firmly. "You really can't." Then he turned back to me again. "Actually you can. Don't come and talk to Aunt Hettie. I know it will make her cross and she'll think we've done something bad and she'll punish us. She may even turn us out."

"But I promised the constable that I'd take you home," I said. "He only let you go because he thought I was now responsible for you. I'll tell your aunt there was a spot of bother on the street and I brought you away for your own safety. I'll also add that I think you're too young to go out alone on the dangerous streets of New York, and let's see what she has to say to that. I may even add that my husband is an important policeman."

"I suppose so." Tig looked decidedly miserable.

We crossed Sixth Avenue in silence and turned onto Christopher Street. I was wrestling mentally with what would be the right thing to do. I was itching to see this aunt and give her a piece of my mind, but a small voice in the back of my mind whispered that my visit might work the wrong way and make her decide to turn the children out onto the street. If she wasn't their legal guardian she'd be under no obligation to give them a home. It was starting to snow harder now, blowing into our faces borne on an icy wind off the river. The children turned up their collars, shoved their hands into their pockets, and trudged miserably toward the waterfront.

We reached West Street and the dockland area of the Hudson piers. Over the roofs of various ramshackle warehouses I caught a glimpse of the funnels of an ocean liner. Seagulls wheeled overhead, crying plaintively. The wind was now bitingly cold and snowflakes swirled. I looked down at little Emmy, shivering in her thin coat, her little cheeks red and raw, and longed to sweep her up and take her home with me right now. Tig trudged beside her stoically, his mouth in a resolute line, clearly worried about what was to happen next.

After two blocks we came to Morton Street.

"That's her house," Tig said. "Do you really have to come and talk to Aunt Hettie? She'll be awfully angry with us."

"I did promise the constable that I'd take you home," I said.

"You did take us all the way home." He chewed on his lip.

I was in an agony of indecision. I so dearly wanted to give that heartless woman a piece of my mind, but I had to consider the consequences from their point of view. If she really did throw them out, I was in no position to take them in. Besides, they were waiting at their aunt's house for their mother to come back.

"If your aunt knows someone is taking an interest in you, she may start treating you better," I said.

"She'll throw us out," Tig said bleakly. "We've nowhere else to go and Mummy wouldn't know where to find us."

Then the situation was decided for me. Liam had been

really good until now, sitting up, strapped into his pram, and watching the world go by. But he had been confined longer than usual and was presumably feeling cold, trapped, and miserable now that wet snow was blowing into his face. He suddenly let out a squeal of frustration and rage.

"Mama. Up," he screamed. "Up. Up." And he reached out to me and he threw himself around, kicking off covers and flailing arms and legs.

Clearly I was in no position for a quiet and calm chat with the aunt with a screaming baby in the background. I supposed I could ask Bridie to push him around for a while, but she also looked so miserable that I didn't want to keep them out in the cold and snow longer than I had to. Liam was reaching the stage when he would become inconsolable. His needs had to come first at this moment. I unstrapped him from the buggy and took him into my arms, attempting to wrap his blanket around him to keep out the icy blast.

"Listen, Tig," I said, turning to the boy. "I'm going to trust you this time and hope that you won't ever let me down. Tell your aunt that there was a disturbance and you had to bring your sister home so that you didn't get involved—all right? And give her the dollar that I just gave you. Tell her an important-looking lady gave it to you and said that she thought you needed a good nourishing meal." When Tig looked skeptical about this I added, "And the lady said she'd come back and check that you'd been fed properly."

"All right." It came out as little more than a whisper.

I had another thought and struggled to open my purse with a wriggling baby in my arms. "And Tig. Can you read?"

"Oh, yes," he said. "Mummy taught me to read when I was Emmy's age. But Emmy hasn't learned properly yet."

"I can read C-A-T," Emmy said. "And D-O-G."

"I'd keep teaching her but we don't have any books," Tig said.

I fished a card from my purse. "Tig, this is my calling card. It has my name and address on it. I live near the Jefferson Market building. That's the building that looks like an old castle. You'll recognize it. If you need me at any time you can come and find me." I handed it to him. "Don't show it to your aunt. It can be our secret."

He took it and tucked it into a pocket.

"Thank you very much," he said. "Come on, Emmy."

He took her hand.

She looked back at me with that angelic smile. "You're a very kind lady," she said, then directed her smile at Bridie, who was busy straightening out the blankets in the pram as the wind whipped at them. "And you're a very kind girl too," she added.

Bridie grinned shyly. "You're welcome," she said. "I'm sorry about your scarf. I hope your mom comes back soon. My dad and brother have gone far away too, and they don't write. But I have Molly and Mrs. Sullivan to look after me."

As they started to walk away, toward the ramshackle house, another thought occurred to me. That young lout who had blamed Tig for the purse snatching. Maybe he was a gang member on the lookout for junior pickpockets and Tig would be a likely recruit, easily threatened or bribed into doing the gang's bidding. "And Tig—" I called, and he turned back to me again. "Come to me if you're in any kind of trouble."

"What sort of trouble?"

"That big boy on the street corner," I said. "The one who told the constable you'd taken the purse. I didn't like the look of him. If he or one of his friends tries to get you to do something bad, you would come and tell me, wouldn't you?"

"I wouldn't do anything bad," Tig said. "But I would come and tell you. I promise."

I put the protesting Liam back into his buggy, much to his dismay, and tried to tuck up his kicking legs. "We're going home," I said. "Going home for din-dins and a nice warm fire."

I let Bridie push him ahead and at the street corner I lingered and looked back. I watched the children go up the front steps. Tig rapped on the door. As I watched, the door opened and a woman appeared. She stood there, hands on hips, head thrust to one side. I could see her mouth moving, but we were too far away to hear what she was saying. Whatever it was, it was angry and hurtful. Then she took Tig by the shoulder and almost flung the children inside before slamming the door. And in spite of everything, I resolved to do what I could to find out the truth about those children and their mother.

✣ Eight ✣

Back at Patchin Place I went about my household tasks, changing and feeding Liam, getting potatoes and carrots peeled for the evening meal, and counting the minutes until Daniel came home. I couldn't get those children out of my mind. I looked at my own son, fat, healthy, laughing as he played with Bridie. Those children had been loved and cared for once by a gentle mother about whom they spoke lovingly. Why would a loving mother ever leave her children to the care of a woman like that one? Where could she have gone? My gut instinct told me that something was very wrong.

I had just made us some tea and toast when Sid and Gus knocked at the front door. They came bursting in with excited faces. "We've been experimenting with fudge. You can be our guinea pigs," Sid said, and held up the plate of fudge balls ranging from dark brown to white, some drizzled with chocolate and some wrapped in chocolate sprinkles.

They went ahead of me into the kitchen. "Look what

we've got, young 'uns," Sid said. "Much more fun than plain old toast."

"Are you sure they are suitable for babies?" I asked. I knew Sid and Gus's way of cooking only too well. The fudge could be half brandy if they had made it.

"Of course," Gus said. "What could be wrong with cream, butter, chocolate, and cocoa?"

"Except for this one," Sid said, pointing at the darkest brown ball. "This one did have a little bourbon in it, remember?"

"Only a little," Gus said with a grin. But she put a pale coffee-colored ball in front of Liam, who took it cautiously and then almost stuffed the whole thing into his mouth.

"Careful." I stopped him just in time. "Take a tiny bite," I warned.

He did so and an expression of wonder came over his face. Wonder and pure delight. We laughed. Bridie was offered one, then I took a bourbon fudge for myself, and poured us cups of tea.

"We thought we'd give these to everyone as Christmas gifts this year," Sid said as I ate mine, almost gasping at the richness and intensity of it. "It saves battling those crowds at the stores, doesn't it? And who could resist?"

"Good idea," I replied. "I haven't made anything yet. My mother-in-law will be arriving in a couple of days and I thought I'd wait until she gets here. She's a much better cook than me and the children will have fun making things like gingerbread men with her."

"But you've made your Christmas puddings, surely?" Gus said.

"No. I haven't."

"But we understood that in Britain it was a tradition to make them on pudding Sunday, last Sunday of November." Sid turned to Gus for confirmation.

I gave an embarrassed chuckle. "At home they were too much of a luxury for us. We'd have a regular steamed pudding with jam on it or currants in it most years. And there was never brandy in our house—my father being the drinker that he was, my mother made sure that he was kept far from all liquor. So I've never really learned to make puddings. But it can't be too late, can it?"

"The brandy won't have as much time to impregnate the fruit but I'm sure it will be all right," Sid said. "We could come over and help. We've never really made a good English plum pudding—just read about them in Dickens."

I reached out to stop Sid from giving Liam a second fudge ball. "He won't want his supper if he eats any more of that," I said. "But they are delicious."

"So what were you doing today?" Gus turned to Bridie, who had been sitting silently until now. "You're looking sad, young lady. What's wrong?"

"We went to see my beggar girl and a mean old lady took away the scarf I had knitted her." Bridie looked as if she might cry.

"Beggar girl?" Sid looked at me. I explained how we had heard the child singing and Bridie had given her some outgrown clothes and knitted her a scarf.

"There are too many people suffering in this city," Sid said. "It breaks my heart to see them every time we go out. Especially the children. But taking away a scarf. That's just downright cruelty. Do they know who this woman was? A gang member?"

"No, it was their aunt—or the woman they call aunt. Their mother left them in this woman's care."

"So there's nothing you can do, is there?" Sid said. "They have a guardian, even if she's a bad one. And they have a place to sleep that's not on the streets, and presumably they are fed. That's a lot better than most, Molly."

"I know." I glanced across at Bridie and sighed. It was better than most but it wasn't good enough.

Sid and Gus took their leave then, saying they had to make the next batch of fudge while they had all the ingredients out and ready. I cleaned up Liam and put him in his playpen in front of the fire, but I couldn't get those children from my mind. Sid was right, of course. If this woman had been assigned as a guardian, then there was nothing I could do. Women beat and abused their children all the time while society looked on. But I couldn't let it go. I had to see that woman myself, to find out what the situation was and where their mother had gone.

Daniel arrived home in time for supper. This was still amazing to me as most of the time we hardly saw him. I was beginning to hope that we'd actually be able to enjoy a real Christmas together for once, without a constable showing up on our doorstep saying that Captain Sullivan was needed urgently.

I served our hot pot and poured Daniel a glass of beer. He was in a good mood, feeding Liam by saying, "Here comes the *choo-choo* train into the tunnel," then bringing the spoon into Liam's opened mouth. Then he turned to Bridie. "And what did you do today, young lady?" he asked. "Did your girl like the scarf you knitted her?"

Bridie had been quiet since we returned home, but she had clearly been brooding on this. Without warning she burst into tears. "The old woman took it away from her," she said between gulping sobs. "And she's so horrible. She yells at them and she shook Tig and their mother has gone away and they don't know when she'll be back . . ."

The words came pouring out in a torrent. I got up and put my arm around her. "It's all right, my darling. Don't cry. We'll try and do what we can."

Daniel was sitting there, his fork poised in midair, looking shocked and mystified. I explained about the children and recounted what had happened. He gave a long sigh. "I'm sorry about the scarf," he said to Bridie. "But there's really nothing we can do. The children have an aunt. They have a place to stay. A roof over their heads."

"That's what Miss Goldfarb said," Bridie said, still sniffing. "I just feel so bad, knowing that they are in a place where nobody loves them and takes care of them."

"You have a kind heart," Daniel said. "But I expect their mother will come back soon and all will be well."

Bridie shook her head. "She's been gone for ages. They don't know where she is."

I still had my arm around her shoulder. "Perhaps we can take them some food—something special. A Christmas treat. And they can eat it while you watch. The aunt can't stop that, can she?"

Bridie nodded, her eyes still brimming with tears. But she got up from the table and lifted Liam from his seat. "I'll get him ready for bed then," she said, and trudged up the stairs with him on her hip.

"Poor little thing," I said when she was gone. "She sees herself in that girl, you know. If it weren't for us she could easily have been on the streets. She could have been living with her cousin Nuala, who would have treated her in the same fashion."

Daniel nodded as he cut himself a hunk of cheese. "It's a hard city, Molly."

"But you know, Daniel," I said thoughtfully as I carried plates over to the sink, "I've been thinking. Those children are so well-spoken, so well-mannered. Is it possible that they have been kidnapped from an upper-class family and brought to this country and this woman is being paid to hold them until the ransom is paid?"

Daniel frowned. "But didn't Bridie say they had come over with their mother?"

I wrestled with this complication. "She might not have been their real mother. What if she was one of the kidnappers, and she told them she was their mother now?"

"Then they wouldn't be sad when she left, would they?"

He was being too darned logical. "There has to be an explanation," I said testily, realizing as I said the words that some of the explanations I'd come up with might sound a little far-fetched. "Something is so clearly wrong. Could you at least look into any recent kidnapping cases? Here and in London?"

"If it was a kidnapping of a society child then it would be in every newspaper in creation," Daniel said.

"What if the family were keeping quiet because the kidnappers threatened to kill the children if they went to the police?"

"Then we wouldn't know about it, would we?" He gave me a slightly patronizing smile that annoyed me.

"Why do you always have to be so right?" I demanded, making him chuckle.

I turned back to my washing up, taking out my frustration by clattering the pots and pans as I washed. I knew very well that my annoyance wasn't with him. It was with myself. I wanted to do something to help but was infuriated with my powerlessness.

Then I remembered something. "There was a pickpocketing incident today," I said. "Just across from Wanamaker's. A woman screamed that someone had taken her purse. The little boy we've been telling you about was accused of doing it by a bigger boy. Of course he was innocent and during the kerfuffle the big boy slipped away. I'm pretty sure he must have taken it himself. But I'd recognize him again, Daniel, and I'm wondering if he might be connected to one of the gangs."

"Probably," Daniel said.

"Don't you want a description of him?"

He smiled. "They are becoming very slick, Molly. Using smaller boys, not connected to a gang, to do the actual dirty work, and the purse is passed down a chain, so that if they are stopped and searched we can never catch them with the stolen purse on them."

"There must be something you can do."

"We have to catch them in the act, like I did yesterday. And we have to make them squeal. Not easy. They're all more frightened of men like Monk Eastman than they are of me."

"Monk Eastman? So you think he's behind this?"

"Wouldn't be surprised."

"Not those Italian ruffians?"

Daniel shook his head. "They'd use Italian boys. The ones we've spotted have been mainly Irish, or English—" He broke off when he saw what I was thinking. "Children can be quite charming and quite devious, Molly, as you'll find when our own son is older. They can look at you as if butter wouldn't melt in their mouths."

"I know," I said. "I raised three brothers. But I'm sure the little English boy was not a thief." And even as I said it, I wasn't sure. If he was somehow mixed up with a gang, if they had threatened him or his sister, wouldn't he do what he was told? Wouldn't the gang be using him just because of his innocent air and well-spoken manners? And that awful woman—Aunt Hettie—might she not be the brains behind a gang of street children, like a New York version of Fagin?

I decided I had to pay a visit to her and see if I could get to the truth.

❧ Nine ❧

Saturday dawned bleak and miserable, with a hard driving sleet that peppered the windows. Not the sort of day one would want to be outside. Although it was Saturday Daniel had to work this weekend, and he left early. As I served Liam and Birdie their porridge my thoughts went to Tig and Emmy. Would they be sent out into this weather, with no proper coats or shawls to keep them warm? I put a pot roast in the oven to cook slowly for us, then I remembered that we had some hot pot left over from the day before. I'd heat it up and take it to the children myself around midday. That way at least they'd have one good meal.

Knowing that my mother-in-law would be arriving the next day, I went about last-minute scrubbing and polishing so that the house would be up to Mrs. Sullivan's standards. The weather was still too miserable at lunchtime for me to want to take the children out, so I put Liam down for his nap and left Bridie to watch him, knowing that she could run across the street to Sid and Gus in an emergency. Then I wrapped the bowl of hot pot in a towel to keep it warm, and put on the long wool cape that Gus had given me. It was nothing like as warm as the cape with a fur-lined hood I'd once owned, but I had lost everything in a fire earlier in the year and was grateful for any donations to my meager wardrobe. I pulled the hood over my hair and set off. It was treacherous going underfoot, with the sidewalks icy and passing carts and carriages sending up sprays of muddy slush. Broadway was suspiciously quiet, the carol singers and bell ringers having been defeated by the elements. But I spotted Emmy in her doorway, hugging her knees to herself, and Tig, standing with the other boys at the crossing, stomping up and down to keep his feet from freezing. I hurried over to them.

"You must be freezing," I said. "I've brought you something to warm you up." And I removed the towel from the bowl. The rich aroma of herbs and vegetables wafted into the air and Emmy's face lit up. I handed her a spoon. "Here, dig in."

"But what about Tig?" she asked.

But Tig was already on his way over to us.

"She brought us food," Emmy called to him. He broke into a trot, almost snatched the spoon I held out for him and started eating as if he hadn't had a meal in weeks. I stood over them, keeping out the worst of the sleet, while they made short work of the stew. Only then did he look up at me. "You are very kind," he said. "I'm sure when our mother comes back she'll be very grateful."

I took the bowl from them and put it back in my shopping basket. I wanted to say something reassuring but I couldn't think of what that might be. That their mother would come back soon? That all would be well? My gaze went to the other boys now busily sweeping at the street crossing. There was probably no happy ending for any of them. The city was full of unwanted children, some of whom would freeze to death tonight or die of starvation tomorrow. As Daniel had said, it was a harsh world. On impulse I went around the corner to a pushcart selling hot potatoes and bought two big ones.

"Here," I said, coming back to Tig and Emmy. "These will help keep your hands warm and then you can eat them."

They took them shyly, murmuring thanks, and I left them huddled together in that doorway. I was headed back home, but then I decided that Liam would be quite safe with Bridie and this might be a good day to have a talk with Aunt Hettie. So I turned and headed down Christopher Street toward the waterfront. The wind blowing off the Hudson was icy and the constable who stood at the corner of West Street looked utterly miserable. I walked past him until I came to the house—one in a row of grimy brick buildings. On the ground floor was a tailor's shop, but beside it was a front door with peeling and faded red paint. The sign on it said *Rooms for Rent.*

On the way over I had been debating how to approach Aunt Hettie. If I expressed criticism about the way she was looking after the children she could throw them out. If I expressed concern she could always tell me to take them in myself. We had no room for that and Daniel certainly wouldn't approve. But now I saw the sign, I decided what I should say. I rapped on the door and after a while heard approaching footsteps. It was opened cautiously, only a few inches, and a suspicious face peered at me.

"Yes?" she said.

"I see you have rooms for rent," I said, putting on my strongest Irish brogue. "Do you have any vacancies at the moment?"

"I might have. For yourself?"

"No. A friend of mine is arriving from Ireland and will need a place to stay until she fixes herself up with a job."

She opened the door wider and I took in the hard face with its jutting chin, perpetual frown, and darting, suspicious eyes. She was a big woman—not fat but big-boned—and she was wearing a dirty apron over a faded wool dress. I could tell she was examining me—my good boots, my thick wool cloak—and wondering what I was doing in this part of the city.

"You'd better come in," she said, and half dragged me into a narrow, dark hallway before slamming the door behind me. I followed her up a flight of stairs. The smell of boiled cabbage grew stronger as we came out onto a landing.

"When will your friend be wanting the room?" She turned to look back at me. "Because Mr. Wilcox is moving out at the end of the week. Going back to Philadelphia, so he says. Doesn't like New York."

"My friend hasn't even sailed from Ireland yet," I said. "She's hoping to get on the next boat out of Queenstown. So it won't be for a couple of weeks at the earliest."

"I can't guarantee to hold a room for her," she said.

"I quite understand that. I was just trying to get a feel of places near the docks. I'd have her to stay with me but I've got a young baby, an older girl, and my mother-in-law with us," I said.

"And what does your man do?"

"He's with the police," I said. Did I detect a slight change in expression? Those eyes now darting even more warily?

"That's a hard job in this weather," she said.

"It certainly is. That poor young constable at the end of your streets looks frozen to the marrow." I let her go on thinking that my husband might also be standing on a street corner at this moment, not sitting in an office at police headquarters.

"The kitchen and dining room are on this floor, together with my own room," she said. "I serve breakfast and dinner, included in the price of the room. The guest rooms are up another flight."

And she started up another flight of dark stairs. On this landing there were four bedrooms, each with the minimum of furniture—a narrow bed, a chest of drawers, a braided rag rug on the floor. They were some of the sorriest rooms I had ever seen and I thought that people would have to be quite desperate to want to stay here. Their occupiers were not present but were all clearly men, from the items of clothing that hung from the bedsteads. It was also clear that the children were not sleeping in any of the rooms here.

"This is the room that will become available," she said as we stood in a narrow back room that looked out onto the brick wall of another building. Washing hung, frozen solid, on the roof opposite, and from one of those windows came the sound of a baby crying.

"I'll pass on the news to my friend," I said. "This is all the rooms you have, is it? Not another floor?"

I had noticed yet another staircase, even narrower this time, going up into darkness.

"That just leads to the attic," she said. "No proper rooms up there—just a storage space under the roof where I keep my odds and ends."

And the children, I thought. *That's where they have to sleep.*

"It's very quiet," I said. "The tenants are all out and working, are they?"

"I don't know if they are working or not. They have to be out during the day. Those are my house rules. I'll not have idlers littering up the place. You'd best make sure your friend knows that."

"I will." I started down the stairs.

I was trying to think how to bring the conversation to the children when she said suddenly, "So how did you hear about me? Live around here, do you?"

"No, I believe that someone must have told me. Was it maybe your sister?"

"My sister?" she demanded sharply. "My sister died when she was eight years old of diphtheria."

"I'm sorry," I said. "Maybe it was another family member."

"That's not likely unless you've come from Ohio," she said. "I've hardly been in touch with my family since I moved here twenty years ago with that no-good husband of mine. He thought he'd make his fortune in New York.

Fortune, huh!" She gave a disgusted grunt. "Hardly call this a fortune, would you. And now he's gone, leaving me to make do as best I can."

I nodded with understanding. "He turned out to be a no-good drunk. I won't allow alcohol on the premises and if any of the men turns up with beer on his breath, I'll not let him in."

As we started down the second flight of stairs I was still searching for a way to mention the children. In desperation I blurted out, "I've remembered who it was," I said. "It was a little boy, sweeping the crossing for me the other day. I asked him if he had a roof over his head and he said he lived at a boardinghouse run by his Aunt Hettie. I asked him where it was and he described the area for me. Am I right—was that you?"

"I've got a couple of young children staying with me at the moment, that's right," she said. "Their mother abandoned them. Walked out one day and never came back. I've kept them here out of the goodness of my heart."

I swallowed back what I'd have liked to say. "That's really Christian of you." I managed to force out the words. "So their mother just upped and left them here?"

"She did indeed. They came off the boat and she rented a room from me. Just for a few days, she said. Then she went out one day and never came back. Only paid rent for a month too."

"That's terrible. What do you think happened to her?"

"In my opinion, she ran off with a fancy man and didn't want children like a millstone around her neck."

"Was she that kind of woman?"

Her face was a stone mask. "I couldn't say. She was a pretty enough little thing. I give her that much."

"Poor little children. So what will happen to them? Have they no relatives they can go to?"

"They came from England," she said, "and from what I understood the father had died and the mother thought they'd be better off over here. She wasn't exactly the talkative sort. Kept herself to herself."

"I wonder why she thought they'd be better off over here?" I said.

I saw I'd gone too far. The suspicious look had returned. "What are you—one of those do-gooders? Poking your nose into other people's business?"

"No, of course not," I said hastily. "But you can't help feeling sorry when you see so many abandoned children in the city, can you? Not when my own children are well fed and loved. But at least you've given these two a roof over their heads, and that's something to be thankful for in this weather."

"It is indeed," she said.

I couldn't stop myself from continuing. "But from what I could see the boy certainly didn't come prepared for our harsh New York winters, did he? Poor little thing looked frozen."

"I house them and feed them," she said, almost spitting out the words. "You're not expecting me to clothe them too, are you? I've no obligation to two strangers."

"Of course you haven't," I said. "Nobody would expect you to do more than you're already doing. But no doubt you'd be glad if I could look through my own girl's things and see if she had any odd bits of outgrown clothing she could spare? We don't have much but I'd like to help if I can."

She hesitated and I could see the wheels of her mind turning. She was wondering whether I was the one who had given the child the scarf and was now checking on it.

"I think it would be most charitable of you," she said.

"It's the spirit of the season, isn't it?" I said, smiling at her. "Makes you want to help those less fortunate."

She didn't answer that one. We had reached the front door. As she opened it a man was coming up the steps toward us. He was a big brute of a man, the type you'd see working on the docks. His hat was pulled down over his face and his coat collar turned up against the cold.

"You're home early, Jack," Hettie said, and I heard sharp tension in her voice.

"Get the kettle on, Hettie," he demanded. "I'm freezing me knackers off." Then he saw me.

"Who's this then?"

"Lady checking out the place."

"Thinking of coming to live here?" He had a coarse round face, cheeks red with cold, but his eyes were also checking me out. I knew when a man was mentally undressing me.

"For a friend," I said quickly. "Coming over from Ireland."

"Oh, Irish, are you? Well, you would be with the red hair. Tell your friend there ain't no better landlady than Hettie here."

He pushed past Hettie and I heard his boots stomping

up the stairs. So much for her rule that tenants weren't allowed in the place during the day, I thought. Or was this one more than a tenant?

"Thanks again," I said, giving her a polite nod. "I'll pass along your information to my friend and bring her to see you when she arrives," I said. "I don't think I'd be looking forward to crossing the ocean at this time of year, would you?"

"I'd not get on a boat," she said. "Not for love nor money. And I didn't catch your name."

"It's Sullivan," I said. "Mrs. Sullivan. And I didn't catch your name either."

She frowned. "Jenkins. Hettie Jenkins. Good day to you then."

As I walked away I permitted myself a little smile. I didn't think it was likely she'd take away any more warm clothing if I found some for the children. And as I stepped back while a brewer's dray came thundering past, it struck me that Jenkins was a Welsh surname. That was interesting, because I suspected that Hettie Jenkins knew more about those children and what had happened to their mother than she was letting on.

On the way home I remembered Sid and Gus's desire to help me with Christmas puddings. Giacomini's was open seven days a week so I went in for dried fruit and spices. My mother-in-law would be arriving tomorrow on the afternoon train, but we'd have time to make the puddings in the morning. As I stepped out of the store and made my way home across Washington Square, the sleet turned to full-blown snow. It started to come down heavily, swirling around and coating me in a white blanket. I was glad when I turned into Patchin Place and opened my front door. Liam had been playing ball in the hallway with Bridie. He took one look at me and burst into tears.

"It's all right," Bridie said. "It's only your mama."

I realized then that I must look like a walking snowman. I threw back the hood and went back to the doorstep to shake off the coating of snow.

"There, is that better?" I asked. "Now it's your mother again."

"You found Tig and Emmy and give them the stew then, did you?" Bridie asked, taking the empty bowl out of my shopping basket.

"I did and they ate up every morsel," I said. "I also bought them each a baked potato to keep their hands warm." I took off my cape and hung it on the hallstand, then I bent to unhook my boots.

"That's good." She tried to smile. "But it's not right they have to be outside on a day like this."

"It isn't," I agreed. "I also went to see the woman they live with."

"And told her to give Emmy back her scarf?"

"Not exactly," I said. "I had to be careful because we don't want her to throw them out, do we?"

"They could come and stay with us," Bridie said.

"That's just not possible," I said. "We have no spare room, for one thing, not with Mrs. Sullivan arriving tomorrow."

"They could share my room," Bridie said.

I laughed. "Three of you squished into one small bed? Besides, Captain Sullivan would never allow it. He says we know nothing about the children and he's quite right. They do have a mother somewhere, and they were left in the care of Mrs. Jenkins."

"Is that Aunt Hettie?" Bridie asked.

"She's not really their aunt. I did gather that much," I said. "But they must have family somewhere. Someone must know where their mother has gone."

"I hope she comes back soon," Bridie said.

"Me too." I picked up Liam and carried him down the hall to the warmth of the kitchen. If she's still alive, I wanted to add. Because the way those children spoke of their mother was with great affection. Surely such a woman would not abandon her children unless there was a very good reason? And the most likely one was that something terrible had happened to her.

I paused, halfway down the hall. I could find out, maybe. After all, I had been a good detective. Then Liam squirmed in my arms and let out a wail of frustration. I gave my own sigh of frustration too: I had a husband, a child, and a ward to look after. And a mother-in-law arriving for Christmas. How could I ever find the time to go poking around New York, looking for a lost woman?

❧ Ten ❧

Sunday

The next morning we awoke to a world of gleaming whiteness. Snow had fallen all night and bushes and garbage cans were now hidden under mantels of snow. Since it was Sunday Gus had not gone to the bakery and the only footprints to spoil the pristine whiteness of Patchin Place were those of the sparrows.

"Thank God for snow," Daniel said as he finished his breakfast and got up from the table. "Always less crime after a bad snowstorm." He looked up and grinned. "They leave telltale footprints behind. And it's harder to run away."

"I don't see why they are making you work on a Sunday if there isn't much crime," I said.

"You know I have to take my turn just like everyone else." he said. "Besides, I've had a fair amount of time off recently, haven't I?"

"I don't want to jinx Christmas by saying you've been home more than usual," I said. "But it's been lovely to have some meals with you."

Daniel made a face. "It might not be all good that I have no major crime to occupy me."

"Why's that?" I detected something in his expression.

"You know the present commissioner doesn't like me. I'm not a Tammany man. It seems to me that he's making sure the juicy cases go to those who are."

I came around the table and put a hand on his shoulder. "He's not around much longer, Daniel. Commissioners are only elected for two years, aren't they?"

"There's such a thing as a second term," he said, looking away from me. "And this one has Tammany in his pocket. They'll make sure everyone votes for him."

"But all your senior officers like you," I said. "You're well respected. You've had great results."

He nodded. "The commissioner apparently thinks I'm too soft on gangs. Just because I'm realistic and understand our limitations. If I tried to crack down the way he wants me to, there would be all kinds of repercussions."

"You did what he wanted earlier in the year and look what happened," I said angrily. "Our house was blown up and poor little Aggie was killed. Do they think that is a satisfactory result?"

He shrugged. "The Cosa Nostra are different. I can work with Monk Eastman. We have developed an understanding. But these Italians—they are violent and brutal and they thumb their noses at the police. I don't know how we'll ever stop them. What's more, they are extending their sphere of influence daily, as more recruits arrive off the boats."

I shuddered, remembering all too clearly the crash of

glass and the explosion that had destroyed our home. I remembered the body of our poor Aggie. "Don't give in to them, Daniel. If anyone can find a way to beat them, you can."

He turned and kissed my forehead. "That's what I like about you, Molly Murphy. Your spunk. You never give in or give up." His eyes traveled over me. "Actually there are more things I like about you—the way that red hair falls over your shoulders when it's not pinned up. That neat little waist. And those lips . . ."

"Don't get carried away," I said, laughing as I held him away from me. "You'll be late for work."

"We'll take this up where we left off tonight," he murmured, giving me the lightest of kisses.

"Your mother will be here," I reminded him.

"Oh, Lord. So she will." He ran his hand through his dark curly hair—something he did when he was worried. "I hope the hansom cabs are able to get around by this afternoon. Did she say what train she was catching?"

"She just said this afternoon," I replied. "Last time she got here around four."

"I'll try and make time to go to Grand Central," he said. "We'll never hear the last if she can't get a cab."

He wrapped a scarf around his neck, put on his cap, and off he went. I went back to clear away the breakfast and get Liam washed and dressed. I set Bridie to writing a note of welcome to put in Mrs. Sullivan's room, but she sat at the table, chewing on her pencil, staring into space and distracted.

"Do you need to know how to spell a word?" I asked.

She shook her head. "I'm thinking of Tig and Emmy. I'm thinking of them out in all this snow."

"I don't expect even Aunt Hettie would be cruel enough to send them out on a day like this," I said, but I wasn't sure at all. I decided to go out and check around lunchtime. I had no leftovers today but I could buy them a baked potato. I went quietly upstairs and looked through my own things. Did I have any garments to spare that could be made into something a child could wear? Since everything I owned had been destroyed in the fire I had only the bare necessities these days. Actually that was a lie—I had several fine silk dresses courtesy of a rich and generous woman, but they were not the sort of clothes for doing housework and looking after babies. It was the sturdy and practical items I lacked. And Bridie had already given Emmy the few things she had outgrown. Who knew if Aunt Hettie had sold those too?

Outside, church bells were ringing, their sound unnaturally clear and sweet against the snowy silence. I felt the usual pang of guilt that I wasn't taking the children to church; I suppose one can never shake off a Catholic upbringing. I made beds, swept the floor, feeling frustration brimming over. Luckily this brooding was interrupted by Sid and Gus, red-cheeked from the cold and eager to make Christmas puddings. Bridie joined in and by the end of the morning we had basins tied up with pudding cloth sitting on the shelf in the scullery. I didn't know how good they would taste, but Sid had been very generous with the amount of brandy she had poured into the mix.

"Now you must come over to us for lunch," Gus said. "Sid has made the most wonderful Tuscan bean soup, full of garlic and herbs. My dears, the place smells like a Continental train carriage!"

"Thank you, we'd love to," I said, taking off my apron.

Bridie wrapped Liam in a blanket to carry him the few yards across Patchin Place. We sat in their warm and cozy kitchen, looking out at the snow-draped world, while Sid dished out ladles of thick and aromatic soup into big bowls.

"I'll feed Liam a little of mine," I said hastily when Sid started on a bowl for him. I didn't want him choking on a bean, and I wanted to test how spicy it was too. Gus poured the adults a glass of red wine to go with it.

"Unfortunately I didn't go to the baker today," Gus said. "I really didn't want to go out in that deep snow. So we've no lovely crusty bread to go with the soup."

I had already taken a spoonful. "It's delicious," I said. I fed some to Liam, who smacked his lips and obviously agreed, leaning forward for more.

We ate in companionable silence. But I couldn't help glancing over at that big iron pot simmering on the stove. "I don't suppose you'd have some of that to share, would you?" I asked.

"Of course. Help yourself," Sid said. "Do you want to take some for Daniel's supper?"

"No, it's not that." I smiled. "Besides, my mother-in-law is supposed to be arriving today, if the train can get through the snow. She wouldn't approve of this much garlic. Actually it's those two waifs I told you about. I hope their unpleasant landlady hasn't sent them out on a day like this, but just in case she has, I'd love to put some warm food in their stomachs."

"Of course, you can take as much as you want." Gus went over to the stove and started ladling soup into a big bowl.

"Just enough for them right now." I held up my hand to stop her. "There would be no point in more than they can eat. It would get cold too quickly and I don't want the landlady to know that someone else is feeding them, or she may stop giving them any food at all."

"So she's a landlady, is she?" Sid asked. "Not a relative? I thought they called her Aunt."

"I went to see her yesterday. A more unpleasant woman you've never seen," I said. "According to her their mother left the children with her, went out, and never returned."

"Then why on earth did the mother leave her children with such a woman?" Sid asked.

"The boardinghouse is close to the docks. It may have been the first one she found . . ." I paused, thinking. "She might not have had much money, and she went to see someone she thought could help her."

"Some kind of family connection, do you think?"

"I don't know. The children speak with an English accent and they came from London. The father was Welsh and he died. I don't know where the mother came from— perhaps she did have family here. She would have to have a compelling reason to bring two small children to America, away from their familiar surroundings, wouldn't she?"

"America, land of opportunity," Gus said. "Maybe with

the father dead she thought she'd have a better chance of finding a job over here."

I shook my head, still trying to make sense of this. "But if you hear the children speak, they sound as if their parents were educated people. It's not as if she'd be looking for a job as a maid or in a factory. So why come here?"

"There must have been someone special she was hoping to contact here. Someone who could help her with the children," Sid said firmly. "When you see them, ask them what their mother told them. Sometimes children take in more than we expect."

"I'll do that," I said. "The unpleasant Mrs. Jenkins suggested that the mother had run off with a 'fancy man' and didn't want the children as an encumbrance."

"It's possible, I suppose," Gus said.

"But the children speak of her with such fondness," I insisted. "I can't believe any mother who loved her children would walk out on them."

"Then something's happened to the mother," Sid said.

"I don't know how we'd ever find out what," I said.

"Do we know their full names?" Gus asked.

"I know their last name is Jones. The boy is Thomas and the girl is Megan. The mother's name is Margaret."

Sid shook her head, making her bobbed hair bounce. "Jones. That won't be easy. How many Joneses are there in the world?"

"But you could check the ship's manifest that brought them here," Gus said. "That might give you some sort of clue. Maybe an address in London?"

"It's worth a try," I said. "I have been feeling so bad that I can't do more. I went through my own clothing, but I have really nothing to give away since our house was burned down."

"We have scarves and shawls in abundance," Gus said. "Happy to find them if you don't think the dreaded Jenkins woman will take them away like she did the scarf that Bridie knitted."

"Maybe the children could sneak them in and hide them somewhere," I said. "That way she'd never know."

"Then let me see what we've got." Gus ran out of the room and I heard her bounding up the stairs. A little later she returned with armfuls of fur and knitted items. "Take your pick," she said, dropping them into a chair.

I had to laugh. "Gus, you are the most generous and the most impractical woman I have ever met," I said. "As if we could give them mink without it being stolen from them in a second." I rummaged through and found a plain black wool scarf. "This would be great for Tig," I said. "And the green shawl for Emmy. She's so tiny it would cover her like a blanket."

"Tig?" Sid asked, looking up from wrapping greaseproof paper around the soup bowl. "Is that his nickname?"

"It seems to be." I examined the scarf and shawl. "Are you sure you want to spare these? They are lovely."

Gus smiled. "We have more things than we need, Molly. Of course you must take them."

"Are you going to take the soup now?" Sid asked.

"Yes, I should take it right away before it gets cold. I can wrap it in the scarves I'm taking them." I looked back at

Liam and Bridie. "But I can't take the children with me on a day like this. And Liam needs to go down for his nap before I dare leave him. So I'd better put him down first . . ."

"They can stay with us until you get back," Gus said. "We'll play with him and make him good and tired!"

"I think I want to go with Molly," Sid said. "I'd like to see the children for myself." She looked up at Gus. "Is that all right with you, if I leave you to take care of the children?"

"You know I adore playing with the children," Gus said. "You go. We'll have a grand time together."

I went home to get my cape. Sid met me, dressed in a double-breasted overcoat and a black beret, looking ridiculously Parisian. We set out. It was not easy going—we were up to our ankles in snow and my feet were soon wet through and miserable. But the thought of those poor children shivering in threadbare and inadequate clothing kept me going. Broadway was unnaturally silent. A few people trudged past, bundled unrecognizably. Shop windows were spattered with snow and the glow of kerosene lamps inside the few that were open on Sundays threw odd patterns onto the snow. But the crossing sweepers were out in almost full force. A narrow path had been scraped clear across Tenth Street and the boys and their brooms stood ready to sweep away the slush for any pedestrian who wanted to cross.

But Tig wasn't one of them. I gave a sigh of relief that Mrs. Jenkins had shown some compassion and not turned them out today. Then I spotted Emmy in her usual doorway. I went over to her. "What are you doing here alone?

Where is your brother?" I asked. My heart was thumping with worry.

"Someone gave him a dime to run an errand," she said. Her eyes went to the things we carried. "Is that food?"

"It is indeed," I said. "And this is my neighbor, Miss Goldfarb, who made this lovely soup."

Emmy's eyes opened wider, then she looked up at Gus and smiled. "Thank you," she said. "You are another kind lady." She took the spoon politely and began to eat.

Sid was staring at her with a look of disbelief. "You must be frozen, you poor little thing," she said. "Have you no warmer clothes?"

"I did have some once," she said. "But I grew too big. And Aunt Hettie must have taken the others away."

"This Aunt Hettie of yours needs talking to!" Sid said angrily. "There should be a law about treating children like this."

"But there isn't, is there?" I said.

"When women have the vote we'll change everything," Sid said. "We'll pass sensible laws. I will have to run for Congress."

We looked up as Tig came running back. His cheeks were bright red from the cold and his breath sounded ragged, coming in bursts from his mouth like a dragon's fire.

"She's brought us more food," Emmy called. Tig needed no urging. He took the spoon he was offered and started shoveling food into his mouth. It was only when he was done that he looked up at Sid.

"This is my friend, Miss Goldfarb," I said. "She made the

soup. And she's brought you things to keep you warm." I held out the shawl and the scarf.

Tig took the scarf, looking up at us with wonder while I wrapped the shawl around Emmy. "I suggest you hide them and don't let Aunt Hettie know you've got them. Maybe you can think of a place where she'd never look."

Tig was wrapping the scarf around his neck and tucking it into his jacket. Emmy was hugging the shawl to her in delight. "It's so warm," she said. "Lovely and warm."

"No," Sid said angrily. They both shrank away, expecting her to want her items back. "I can't leave you out here in this weather. I simply can't. Come on. I'm taking you home with me right now."

Tig looked at her uncertainly. "But I'll lose my patch sweeping here if we go away. And we don't know you. Mummy said we weren't to go with strangers."

"Miss Goldfarb is a very kind woman," I said. "And she's right. Nobody should be outside on a day like this."

"I suppose so," Tig said, looking at Emmy for confirmation. "I already made a dime for running that errand. Aunt Hettie can't expect more money than that on a day like this, can she?"

We started the walk home, each of us holding a child's hand. "So why did you come to America, Tig?" Sid asked as we came to Fifth Avenue. "Do you have relatives here?"

"I'm not sure. There is somebody," Tig said. "Mummy was sick for a long time and then Daddy died, so we were all alone in London. So Mummy said that things would be better in America and we'd have someone to take care of us."

Oh, I thought with sinking heart. Mummy had been sick for a long time. Perhaps their mother knew she was dying and wanted to see that her children were safe somewhere. But perhaps the end came quicker than she had planned, and she never managed to get in touch with the person she thought could help her.

"Did your mother say where this relative was? Did she mention a name?" I asked him.

Tig frowned, then shook his head. "I don't think so. She said she'd be gone for a little while and then everything would be all right for us. But she hasn't come back yet and it's been ages and ages." He looked up at Sid with a desolate face. "And she doesn't even write."

"We're going to do everything we can to try and find your mother, Tig," I said.

"How?" he asked.

"This lady was a real-life detective," Sid said. "She's good at finding lost things."

"Really?" He looked up at me, more hopefully now.

I nodded, giving him an encouraging smile, even though an inner voice was whispering that I had no time to search out lost relatives at this moment.

"So was your mother American, Tig?" Sid asked. "Did she come from here?"

"I don't know." He looked at Emmy for confirmation.

"Did she speak like the other people in London or more like people here?"

He wrinkled his nose, trying to remember. "Not like my father. He had a different way of speaking. But not like Aunt Hettie either. More like you, miss." He looked up at Sid.

"She has a soft, gentle voice. She used to read us stories and sing to us."

"Emmy has a beautiful singing voice," I said, looking down at the little girl who was holding my hand. "You must hear her sing Christmas carols."

"Gus can play the piano for you," Sid said.

"Who is Gus, your husband?" Emmy asked.

"She's my friend," Sid said with a smile. "You'll like her. She's also very sweet and gentle, like your mom."

Tig was frowning, stomping silently through the snow. I suspected he was worried about going home with a stranger, however nice we seemed. I remembered what Daniel's reaction had been when I told him about the beggar children—that people are not always what they seem. That the sweetest-looking children are sometimes the biggest scoundrels. In truth we did know so little about them. I just hoped Sid was not making a mistake, bringing the children into her house.

"We're almost home," Sid said as we approached the Jefferson Market building.

"Oh, that's the castle you told us about," Tig said, finally showing some animation. "We went to see the Tower of London once."

"Did you go down to the dungeons?" Sid asked.

"Yes, we did."

"And were you scared?"

"A little bit."

"So was I," Sid said.

"You've been to London?" Tig asked.

"Several times. It's fun, isn't it? Where did you live?"

"We lived near the river. My daddy worked at the docks."

"I thought you said he was a singer," I said.

"He was. But it's hard to find work singing and sometimes he didn't make much money. Then Mummy got sick and we had to pay doctor's bills, so my daddy went to work loading ships. That's how he got killed. Something fell on him."

"How very sad," I said. "Your poor mother, with two little children and no relatives nearby."

"She cried for a long time," Emmy said.

We turned into Patchin Place.

"Is there anything else you can tell us about your mother that might help us find her again?" Sid asked.

"She had a pony," Emmy said. "When she was a little girl she had a pony called Squibs."

"Anything more? Did she talk about her brothers or sisters?"

Tig shook his head. "She didn't like to talk about it because it made her sad."

"Mrs. Sullivan!" A voice yelled behind us and footsteps echoed, unnaturally loud, against the silence of the snow. I turned to see a constable running toward me. His face was familiar and I remembered he'd been sent to deliver messages to Daniel before.

"What is it, Constable Byrne? If you're looking for Captain Sullivan, he's not here," I said.

"You have to come right away, Mrs. Sullivan." He gasped out the words. "There's been a shooting. Captain Sullivan has been shot."

✤ Eleven ✤

The world stood still.

"He's been shot?" I forced out the words. "Where is he? What happened?"

"It was not too far from police headquarters on Mulberry Street. One of the new guys thought he'd go and arrest one of the big shots in the Cosa Nostra—the Italian gang, you know?"

"I know," I snapped, fear and frustration boiling over.

"And the captain heard about it and went to stop him. And there was shooting . . ." He looked as if he might burst into tears himself.

"Is he dead?"

"I don't know, ma'am. I saw them putting him into an ambulance. He wasn't moving and there was a lot of blood, and I came running to get you. I knew you'd want to be with him."

"Where have they taken him?"

"St. Vincent's, ma'am."

"Then I must go to him."

I looked at Sid. "Don't worry," she said. "We'll keep the children with us. You go."

"I don't think we'll find a hansom cab," I said. "It's probably quicker on foot. At least it's not too far from here."

"I'd like to come with you, Mrs. Sullivan, but I'm on duty. I shouldn't have left in the first place, but the captain has been good to me and I knew you'd want to know straight away."

"That's all right, Constable. I can find my own way to St. Vincent's," I said. "You were good to tell me. I just hope . . . I just pray . . . he's still alive when I get there."

"The captain—he's tough, ma'am. He'll pull through if anyone can."

He went to say something more, then took off, half running, half slithering, back along the snowy sidewalk. Sid was already shepherding the two children down Patchin Place. I picked up my skirts and headed up Greenwich Avenue. My numb and frozen feet burned within my boots. The icy wind stung my cheeks. I found it hard to breathe but I didn't stop. "Must get there in time," I chanted over and over, mixed with the prayer, "Holy Mother of God, please let him live. Please let him live."

The hulking building of St. Vincent's Hospital loomed ahead of me as I turned onto Seventh Avenue. I staggered in through the main door and was met by a sister in a crisply starched veil and uniform.

"Where are you going, my dear?" she asked in broader Irish than my own, grabbing my sleeve as I went to push past her.

"My husband. Where is he?" I asked. "Where have they taken him?"

"Your husband? What's his name, my dear? Brought into casualty, was he?"

"Captain Sullivan. A policeman. He was just shot. They were taking him here."

"We've nobody just arrived who has been shot," she said. "Maybe he's still on his way. It's not easy for an ambulance to get through in this snow, you know." She took my arm and started to lead me. "You look as if you're about to pass out. Come on in and I'll get you a cup of tea." She led me through to a plain scrubbed kitchen and sat me at a bench while she poured me tea. I took a grateful sip, realizing that my hands were shaking. What would I do without him, I thought. How would I survive? I'd be like that poor woman who brought her two children to America because she had nobody to turn to in London. Then I made myself calm down and see sense. I did have people who cared for me. I had Sid and Gus and Daniel's mother . . . it wouldn't be the same for me at all. It was just that I couldn't bear to think of life without him.

The Italian gang. The stupid Italian gang. Daniel had warned his fellow officers that they were not to be trifled with, neither could they be stamped out. But nobody had listened to him and it had cost him . . . The sister stood up, her head cocked like a bird's. "Ah, that sounds like horses' hooves," she said. "That will be them now. And our doctors here are first-rate. So don't you worry. They'll save him if anyone can."

I followed her out to a side entrance and watched the ambulance come to a halt under the portico, the two horses' breath still coming like smoke and their flanks steaming. Two orderlies had come out to open the back door of the wagon. The driver climbed down from his perch. "Policemen," he said. "Been shot."

I hung back. The orderlies climbed inside the wagon and then one of them jumped down and between them out came a stretcher, and it was covered in a white cloth.

"Didn't make it," the orderly said as the driver came around to assist. "Looks like he was shot through the heart. Nothing we could do. I think he was killed outright on the spot."

I put my hand to my mouth to stifle the sob. I was shaking all over now, vaguely aware that the sister had put an arm around me. "You'd better come inside out of the cold," she said.

"Put that stretcher down and give me a hand with the other one," someone shouted from within the wagon. "We need to get him into the operating theater before he loses any more blood."

They scrambled back into the wagon and lowered a second stretcher. I saw Daniel's dark curls, his face deathly white, one hand hanging lifelessly over the side of the stretcher. I shook myself free of the sister and ran up to him.

"Daniel, my darling. It's me, your Molly is here. You're going to be just fine," I babbled as I walked beside them.

"Stand out of the way, please, ma'am," one of the stretcher-bearers said. "We're taking him into surgery. You can't come with us."

One of them had opened double doors. I caught a glimpse of a long white corridor stretching away.

"Daniel, I love you," I called. The doors swung shut behind them. The sister led me to a waiting room and brought me another cup of tea. Other people were sitting around the walls, but in truth I hardly noticed them. I could not say how many or how old they were. They were just a vague blur of color against the pale green of the walls and the gray linoleum on the floor. It was horribly cold and the disinfectant smell wafted in from the corridor. I couldn't stop shaking and the teacup rattled against the saucer in my hand. Did people survive gunshot wounds? I had been there when President McKinley had been shot. He had lived for a few days and then died anyway.

Daniel's tough. I repeated the constable's words. *He'll make it if anyone can.* The clock on the wall ticked annoyingly loudly. Feet tapped up and down hallways, just out of sight. Other people were called out of the room until there were just one or two of us, sitting wrapped in our own cocoons of misery. Time dragged on, minute after painful minute. Then finally I heard heavier footsteps approaching. A man in a white coat appeared—a young man with red hair and a freckled face, looking ridiculously young to be a doctor.

"Mrs. Sullivan?" he said.

I jumped to my feet. "Is he . . . ?" I couldn't finish the sentence.

"Your husband is a lucky man," he said. "The bullet passed through his shoulder, just missing his heart and his lungs. It went clear through him and out the other side. So we didn't even have to dig around to find it." He even smiled. "He's lost a lot of blood, but we've patched him up and dressed the wound and with any luck he'll be fine."

A great sob escaped from my throat. I put my hand to my mouth. "Can I see him?" I managed to say.

"We're transferring him to a ward right now. When he wakes up and he's settled you'll be able to see him."

"I'm glad it was good news, my dear," said a gentle voice from across the room, and I noticed, really for the first time, that an old woman sat there. She was dressed in an aged, moth-eaten fur coat and held rosary beads in her hands.

"Thank you," I said.

"My own dear Timothy was brought in with pneumonia," she said. "It came on so quickly. Fighting for his life, they said. I don't know what I'll do without him. We've been married fifty-one years."

I went over to her and took her hand. "It's a good hospital," I said. "He's in the best hands."

"He's in God's hands," she said. "I can't tell you how many times I've said this rosary as I've been sitting here. Would you like to say it together with me, one more time? They say when two or three are gathered in His name God will answer our prayers, don't they?"

And so I prayed the rosary with her. It had been years, since the nuns had taught me at St. Brendan's, that I'd prayed a rosary. But the old familiar words slipped off my tongue as if it was yesterday. And I did find it comforting. Maybe I had stayed away from the church because of my unhappy experiences with priests and nuns, and my hostility had nothing to do with God. Maybe He had been there, unchanging, all the time.

Outside I heard a clock chiming four. Incongruous thoughts flashed through my head: My son wouldn't have had his nap. And my mother-in-law would be arriving to an empty house. Surely she'd have the sense to knock at Sid and Gus's front door and find out what had happened. Why was it taking so long for Daniel to regain consciousness and to get settled in a ward? Finally I could stand it no longer. I got up and wandered out into a hallway. A young sister came out of a side room. I hurried after her. "Please, can you find out where they have taken my husband," I said. "I want to see him."

"Your husband?"

"The policeman brought in with a gunshot wound?"

"I expect he was taken to the morgue, ma'am," she said.

"No, he was alive. The doctor said he was going to be all right," I insisted.

"Oh, I'm sorry. I didn't realize there were two of them. If they are through with him in surgery they'll have taken him to Saint Luke—the men's surgical ward. It's up one flight of stairs and to the right."

I set off, my feet echoing from the high stairwell. I had just found the men's surgical ward when a nurse came out.

"Have they brought Captain Sullivan up to this ward yet?" I asked as she started to walk past me. "The policeman with the gunshot wound."

"Yes. They brought him in a little while ago."

"Thank you," I said. As I made for the door she added

sharply, "But visiting hours ended at four. You'll have to come back tomorrow. Noon to four."

I had had enough of being patient. I spun to face her. "My husband has been shot and nearly died. If you think I'm going to wait until tomorrow to visit him, you've got another think coming." Then I stalked past her and into the room.

I heard her saying, "But he shouldn't be disturbed . . ." but I didn't wait to hear the rest. I didn't wait to see if she was following me. It was a long ward, with at least twelve beds on either side. Some patients were bandaged so that it was impossible to recognize them. I walked slowly, examining each bed, but didn't see Daniel in any of them. One of the beds at the far end had a screen around it. I peeked around the screen and saw Daniel lying there, his face almost as white as the pillow behind him. His eyes were closed and he looked so peaceful that for a second I thought he must be dead. Then I saw the sheet gently rise and fall with his breathing. I tiptoed up to him and took his hand. It was awfully cold and I held it tightly in mine. I perched on the side of his narrow bed, looking at him.

Winter darkness started to fall outside the high windows and the long ward melted into gloom. Daniel had not stirred. I decided that I would have to go. He was safe here and my son and mother-in-law needed me. But I wanted him to know that I'd been here. Outside the screen I heard the clatter of a trolley. A young orderly pulled back the screen and I watched her react with surprise.

"What are you doing here?" she whispered. "Visiting hours were over long ago."

"I'm Mrs. Sullivan. My husband was brought in with a gunshot wound."

"Ah, yes. The policeman." Her expression softened. "But he's been given morphine. The best you can do for him is let him rest."

"I know. But when he wakes can you tell him I was here? And I'll be back tomorrow."

"Of course," she said. "Don't worry. We'll take good care of him."

As I gently released his hand his eyes fluttered open.

"Molly?" he murmured.

"I'm here, my darling. You're going to be just fine."

"That damned fool," he muttered. "What was he thinking? They don't understand . . ."

"Don't try to talk now," I said, bending to kiss his forehead. "I have to go back to Liam and your mother. But I'll be back in the morning."

His eyes were closed again but he smiled.

"And you have to hurry up and get well for Christmas," I said. "We have to buy Liam's present."

"Dog," he said. "Dog on wheels."

"That's right. A dog on wheels. We'll go to buy it when you're well again."

But he had already drifted back into sleep. I let the orderly lead me out and I found my way down the stairs and out into the street.

❧ Twelve ❧

I wasn't sure what I'd find when I arrived back at Sid and Gus's house. Liam in hysterics with a soaked diaper? My mother-in-law looking indignant and uncomfortable? But complete quiet reigned as Sid opened the door to me.

"What news?" she asked.

"The doctors think he will live, thank God," I said. "The bullet just missed his heart and lungs. It went right through his shoulder and out the other side. But he's awfully weak and they've given him morphine. So he's sleeping peacefully."

"Well, that's good news," Sid said.

"Where are the children?" I asked.

She glanced across the street. "Your mother-in-law arrived, quite put out that you weren't home until we told her the reason. She's taken Bridie and Liam back to your house to put him down for a nap and to cook your dinner. And Tig and Emmy have gone back to the witch. I told them they could stay longer, have an evening meal with us and then I'd walk them home, but they were afraid they would get into trouble if they didn't show up at the proper time.

They were so pathetically grateful, Molly. They perched on the edge of the sofa as if they were afraid to damage it. Not like children at all. Even when I got out games for them, they didn't want to play."

"They've had their childhood taken away from them," I agreed. "They've lost all security and hope, haven't they?"

"And that awful woman. Honestly, Molly, I didn't want to let them go back to her, but they are terrified their mother will come looking for them and they won't be there."

"Did they tell you anything more that might give us a clue as to where she went or why they are here?" I asked.

Sid shook her head. "Not really. But I did gather that the ship they came on was the SS *New York*. That's the American Line, isn't it? So we may be able to glean some information from the ship's manifest."

"Good idea," I said. "I can't thank you enough for helping out like this, and it was so kind of you to bring Tig and Emmy home with you."

Sid glanced back down the hall. "Gus and I have been talking and we think we'd like to take them in."

"You mean bring them to you every day?"

"No, I mean have them to live with us."

"Oh, no, Sid," I said. "I don't think that's wise at all."

"Why? You don't think they are trustworthy? You think they are not what they seem and will murder us in our beds when we're not looking? Or steal the silver?" She sounded indignant now.

"We know nothing about them, Sid. They seem like adorable children and my instinct tells me that they are exactly who they claim to be. But taking them in is another matter. And Tig is right. What if their mother comes to collect them at the boardinghouse and they are not there? That old witch would not tell her where they had gone, just out of spite, I know it." I could feel the blood rising in my cheeks as the frustrations and worries of the day all boiled over. "And what if their mother is never found? What then? Turn them out onto the streets again?"

"Of course not . . ." she started to say, but I went on, "So you'd take them on for the long term? Adopt them? But what would that do to your way of life? You couldn't just jump on a boat to Paris anymore, or go to Newport because it was too hot in the city. And you know nothing about raising children . . ."

Sid put a hand on my shoulder. "Molly, calm down. We're not thinking too far into the future. Just far enough so that they don't have to be out on these freezing streets. If the weather gets better and their mother still hasn't turned up, maybe you'll have found a family connection by then. If not . . . then we'll face that when it comes."

I took a deep breath. "I think you're both kindhearted," I said. "And I see nothing wrong with taking them in during the worst of the weather, as long as you let them go back to the boardinghouse at night."

"But they sleep up in the attic there," Sid said. "Emmy told me they are so cold and they lie on a straw pallet and it's scratchy. And there are mice and she's scared. We could make sure they are warm and well fed, Molly. And you can use your brilliant detective skills to find their mother."

"In case you've forgotten, I've a seriously injured husband to look after as well as two children and a visiting mother-in-law," I said. "I don't know how much time I'll have."

"You'll find time. You always do," Sid said. When I nodded she put a hand on my shoulder. "You do want to help those children, don't you? We can't just turn our backs on them, Molly. We have to do something for them."

"I know," I said. "I want to help them. Of course I do."

"We'll help you find their mother," Sid said. "You tell us what you want us to do and we'll do it."

"You could start off by taking a look at the ship's manifest," I said. "At least we'd know the mother's full name then, and maybe even an address we could contact."

"I'll do that tomorrow," Sid said. "Gus can collect the children and amuse them and I'll go hunting."

"That's a good start," I said. "And if only Daniel weren't lying at death's door he could tell me how to find a list of women who died in the city back in the spring. Maybe women who were found on the streets, or died in an accident. Of course if their mother had been very ill and was taken to hospital and died, then we'd have to go around all the hospitals, wouldn't we? But it can be done."

"You think she's dead, do you?" Sid asked.

"I can't think of any other reason that a mother would not return to her children; would not at least write to them, to let them know she's all right and thinking about them."

Sid nodded gravely. "Yes, I suppose you are right."

"I have to go," I said. "Daniel's mother will be wanting news of him."

I turned away and crossed the street to my front door. Daniel's mother appeared from the kitchen, wearing an apron, her hands floury, but her eyes anxious.

"Molly—what news, my dear?" she asked.

"He's still alive. They think he'll make it just fine." Then to my utter embarrassment I burst into tears. She came up and put her arms around me, patting my back awkwardly.

"My poor dear girl. Don't cry. It will be all right."

"I hope so," I sniffed between sobs.

She led me down the hallway and took off my coat and hat as if I was a child. "I've made us a cup of tea and some of those jam tarts that Liam likes so much," she said as she sat me down at the kitchen table and went to pour me a cup of tea.

"There. Get that down you." She put the cup down in front of me and pushed a plate of still-warm tarts across the table to me.

I drank, gratefully, the sweet hot liquid bringing warmth back to my body.

"Where's Liam?" I asked.

"I put him straight to bed," she said. "He was overtired and overstimulated by the time I picked him up. Your friends don't realize that babies can't take too much excitement. I couldn't quieten him myself. It took Bridie lying down with him on her bed. She's certainly got a way with him, hasn't she? But he's asleep now and she's sitting in his room, keeping an eye on him."

"Thank you," I said. "I was so worried about leaving them that long, but I didn't want to leave Daniel either."

"Of course you didn't. So tell me all about it. I only got the bare bones from your neighbors. Only that he'd been shot."

"That's right," I said. "From what I've been told he found out that a new officer had taken it upon himself to arrest one of the leaders of the Cosa Nostra—you know, that's the Italian gang who have been causing such trouble."

"The ones who bombed your house?"

"That's them. And Daniel went after this man because he knew it was going to cause more harm than good. They must have walked into an ambush. The other policeman was killed. Daniel was lucky. The bullet went clear through his shoulder."

"Praise the good Lord for that," Mrs. Sullivan said.

"But he's lost a lot of blood. They've given him morphine and he's sleeping. I'll take you to see him tomorrow."

"He's strong. He'll pull through, with the good Lord's help," she said, more to convince herself than me, I suspect.

"Of course he will," I agreed. We sat there, looking at each other.

"He'll be home and we'll have a grand Christmas," she said firmly. She got up and went over to the shelf. "I've brought a Christmas pudding. And I've made mincemeat ready for pies. And some candied peel and sugar plums." She stopped and looked up. "Oh, but I see you've made a pudding yourself."

"I thought I'd give it a try," I said. "I don't know how successful it will be. I'd never made one before. I'm sure yours will be much better."

"Well, two puddings are always better than one," she said, but I could tell she was trying to hide her annoyance. "By the way, who were those strange children at your neighbors' house?"

"They were two little beggar children we found on the street. Bridie felt sorry for them, and now we're going to try and find their mother."

"It's not wise to take in street children." Mrs. Sullivan shook her head. "You don't know anything about them."

"Well, these ones came from England and they have obviously been raised well. Their manners and way of speech are beautiful. And you should hear the little girl sing."

"So how did they get here? Do you think they were kidnapped?"

"It's a big mystery," I said. "I was hoping that Daniel could help me locate their mother. According to them she brought them to America, then one day she went off and left them at an awful boardinghouse. And she never came back."

"Dear me. What a tragedy." She poured herself a cup of tea and brought it back to the table. "So many sad stories in a city like this, aren't there?"

"At least we can do a little to help these children," I said. "Sid and Gus plan to take them in and feed them, and I'm going to try and look into why they came to America and whether they might have family here."

"You're a good woman, Molly," Mrs. Sullivan said. "But don't let your heart go ruling your head. You've your own child to care for, and who knows how much attention your husband will need as he recovers."

"I know." I stood up and managed a smile. "I'd better get on with our dinner," I said. "I'd planned a lovely meal for us all. Daniel has been coming home at a good hour and I thought . . ." I pressed my lips together. "Never mind. He'll be home soon."

❧ Thirteen ❧

I found it hard to sleep that night, alone in the big bed without Daniel's comforting body beside me. Every time I turned over and felt the cold space where he normally lay, the worry would surface again. The doctor said the gunshot had missed vital organs and he was going to be all right. But he'd lost a lot of blood. And what about gangrene? Wasn't that always a danger with wounds? And would he recover full health, able to return to work? What if he didn't? And then those worries mingled with thoughts of Tig and Emmy. How could I hope to trace their mother now, when I had so much on my plate and so many worries?

The night seemed to stretch on and on. On Monday morning I wanted to go to see Daniel, but I didn't think the hospital would let me flaunt visiting hours twice. So I busied myself with my normal routine, making breakfast, bathing Liam, getting a load of his diapers out on the line. It was a sparkling bright day so I bundled up the two children and let them play in the snow outside in the street. I found Sid and Gus just emerging from their front door.

"The children didn't come here like we told them to," Sid said. "So Gus is going in search of them and I'm going to the shipping company's office."

"I hope they are all right," Gus said. "I'm just worried that they got into trouble with Aunt Hettie for coming to our house yesterday. I did warn them not to tell her, but you know how children are."

"She might even have spies on the street who reported them," I said, bending to pick up Liam, who had slithered onto his bottom and was lying on his back, looking helpless and surprised.

"I wish we could get them away from that woman." Gus shook her head. "If they do show up here while we're out, please take care of them, won't you?"

"Of course."

"And when will you be going to see Daniel?"

"Visiting hours aren't until noon. I got into trouble for creeping into the ward after hours yesterday so I'd better obey the rules today," I said.

"If Tig and Emmy come, you can show the children how to build a snowman," Gus said to Bridie as she turned to leave.

"I think Tig and Emmy would rather be inside, out of the snow, don't you?" Bridie muttered to me as Sid and Gus went off down the street. "They have enough snow every day."

"You're probably right," I agreed.

"We could start on a snowman anyway," Bridie said. "Will you help?"

"Why not?" I laughed and we started to roll a ball of

snow. We had a good-sized first ball when Bridie looked up and said, "Here they come now!"

Tig and Emmy were running toward us. There was no sign of Gus.

"Well, here you are after all," I said. "Miss Walcott went to look for you. Did something keep you?"

"We weren't going to come," Tig said. "It didn't feel right coming here. We have to take home money or Aunt Hettie will be angry."

"I'm sure Miss Walcott and Miss Goldfarb would be happy to give you some money," I said, looking at his worried face.

"We can't keep accepting things," Tig said. "Mummy wouldn't think that was right. And it's not too cold today. So we went back to our usual patch. Then the big boy asked me to run an errand again for him and said he'd give me a dime. So I ran the errand and there was this pawnshop. And I looked in the window and . . . And I saw Mummy's locket."

"Your mother's locket was in a pawnshop window?" I asked. "Are you sure it was hers and not one like it?"

He nodded. "I know it was hers. It has her initials on it. So I thought she must be in the city right here somewhere, because she never took her locket off."

I looked around, hoping that Gus might be coming back, then made a decision. "We'll leave the snowman until later. Liam's probably had enough snow for one day. Let's go inside and get warm, and then I'll leave Emmy here while Tig and I go and look at this locket."

I peeled off their cold, wet outer layers, then introduced the children to Mrs. Sullivan.

"How do you do, ma'am," Tig said, holding out his hand solemnly. "Pleased to meet you."

Emmy smiled shyly when offered a jam tart. She took a bite. "These are very delicious," she said. "You're a good cook."

Mrs. Sullivan gave a surprised smile, then looked up at me.

"Do you mind keeping an eye on the children while I take Tig?" I said. "He's found his mother's locket."

"You do what you have to do," Mrs. Sullivan said. "I'm sure the little girl will be no trouble. And it will do Bridie good to have another girl to play with."

So Tig and I set off. Instead of heading north to the corner opposite Wanamaker's where Tig swept his street crossing, he directed me south when we came to Broadway.

"Your errand was quite a distance," I said. "Were you delivering a letter?"

"No, not a letter," he said. "Just a package. Nothing special."

I glanced at him. The offhand manner of speaking was not like him. For a moment I found myself wondering whether the nice manners and innocent demeanor were only an act. But then we turned onto Houston Street and on the corner of the Bowery was the pawnshop. Tig hurried ahead of me, scared, I think, that the locket would have disappeared. But he pointed excitedly at the window.

"There it is. Right at the front on that black-velvet pillow. See."

It was a pretty oval gold locket, almost an inch long. There was a delicate row of tiny seed pearls around the border and on the face three letters had been engraved. I read them, an *M*, an *E*, and an *M*.

"Do you know what the letters stand for, Tig?" I asked.

He shook his head. "Her name is Margaret, that's all I know."

"Come on," I said. "Let's go and find out."

I pushed open the door and stepped into the pawnshop. Inside it was dark and smelled musty. An elderly Jewish man came out of a back room. "Good morning, madam. And how can I help you today?" he asked. He spoke English with a strong European accent.

"You have a locket in your front window."

"Ah, yes. Pretty little thing, isn't it? I've only just put it out. You're in luck."

"Might I see it, please?"

"Of course." He went and slid open the window backing, reaching past a violin, a pair of Chinese dogs, and a leather briefcase to retrieve the velvet pillow. He brought it over to me and put it on the glass counter. "Here it is. Twenty-two-karat. And fine workmanship too."

"Would you be able to tell me when this locket was brought to your store and who pawned it?"

"I am only employed here, not the store owner," he said. "He should have all the details. But I can tell you it must have been brought in more than three months ago, or it wouldn't be in the window for sale. We give the customers three months' grace to retrieve their objects."

"And how can I find out who pawned the item in the first place?" I asked.

He was looking at me warily now. "Is there any suspicion that it might have been stolen?" he asked. "We run a respectable shop here. If we'd thought it was stolen we would never have accepted it."

"It belongs to this boy's mother," I said. "He recognized it in the window. But his mother is missing and we are trying to trace her. She may well have pawned it herself, intending to retrieve it again."

"I see." He peered over the counter at Tig. "You think it looks like your mother's locket, do you, son?"

Tig nodded. "I'm sure it's her locket," he said.

The man went on staring, then he said, "I can go and ask the boss what he remembers. He's upstairs in his apartment, if you can wait a moment."

And he disappeared through a back door. The locket lay there on the pillow. I had an absurd desire to grab it and flee with it. But Tig and I stood like statues until we heard the heavy tread of feet coming down stairs again. The man reappeared. "The boss does remember. It wasn't a woman who brought in the locket," he said. "It was a man."

"A man?" My worst fear was being confirmed. Mrs. Jenkins had suggested that Tig's mother had run off with a "fancy man." Perhaps she had good reason to say this. Perhaps she had seen them together. After all, her husband had died. What better reason to come to New York than to meet up with a former love? But abandoning her children? What mother would ever do that?

"Do you have a name for this man?" I asked.

"He said it was an older man. A rough type," he said.

"He doesn't have the card any longer because the piece was not retrieved in the proper time. But he thought the name might be something like Hobson."

"Hobbs?" Tig exclaimed. "It sounds like Uncle Jack."

We both turned to him. "Uncle Jack? Who is he?"

"He's a man who lives at Aunt Hettie's house," Tig said, his face red and animated now. "His name is Mr. Hobbs, but she said we should call him Uncle Jack."

"I think I met him," I said before I realized that I had not told the children I'd paid a secret visit to their Aunt Hettie. Tig looked at me questioningly.

"I went to see your horrible aunt," I said. "Oh, don't worry. I pretended I wanted to rent a room from her. But this man Hobbs was coming in as I was leaving. A most unpleasant fellow if ever there was one."

Tig nodded. "Aunt Hettie is very friendly with him. We can hear them talking and laughing together late at night. But he's horrible too. We heard him saying once that she'd been good to us for too long and it was about time she got rid of us."

"And what did she say?" I asked.

"She said he knew why she couldn't do that yet."

"So the locket belonged to this lad's mother, but it was his uncle who brought it in?" the man asked impatiently.

"I think it's highly likely that they stole the locket from this boy's mother," I said. "He's not really their uncle, I'm sure. Neither is the woman they call Aunt Hettie really their aunt. They could well be criminals. My husband is a police captain and I'll have to tell him about this. I'm sure you wouldn't want to be accused of accepting stolen goods."

"Of course not," he said hastily. "But we definitely accepted the locket in good faith. And what proof do you have that the locket belongs to this boy's mother?"

"Her initials are on the outside," I said.

"And inside there are two locks of hair," Tig blurted out, stepping up to the counter now and trying to grab the locket. The pawnbroker picked it up before Tig could take it and clicked open the catch. Inside, behind a glass compartment, were two locks of white-blond hair, one tied with a blue ribbon, one with pink.

"They were from Mummy and her brother when they were babies," he said, "but she said they looked just like mine and Emmy's."

"I guess the young man does recognize the piece then," the man said. "That is pretty conclusive, I'd say. So the question is, what do we do now? If a relative brought it in, then it hardly counts as stolen. It's more a family dispute, I'd say."

"He's not a real relative," I said. "This boy and his mother arrived recently from England. They were staying in a boardinghouse and the children were left in the custody of the landlady while the mother had to go away. The children refer to this woman as Aunt Hettie, and the woman's friend as Uncle Jack, but in no way are they related. In fact I strongly suspect they went through his mother's things while she was gone, and helped themselves."

The man frowned. "The problem is that my employer loaned out good money for this. In good faith."

"I'd be prepared to buy it if you offer me a fair price," I said. "That way you would be spared any embarrassment if his mother returns and finds her locket is missing, and has been stolen and pawned."

He paused then, weighing this up. "It is a piece of the best quality," he said. "I couldn't let you have it for less than ten dollars."

I thought of Christmas coming, and my husband in hospital, and the need for money to buy presents. "I'm a policeman's wife," I said. "And my husband is currently in a hospital bed, having been shot by a gang. Ten dollars is above my means, I'm afraid. But I simply can't leave the locket here to be purchased by a stranger. I suppose I could manage five dollars now, and if we find proof that the locket was stolen, then we'll say no more about it. And if it wasn't . . . then I'll pay you the rest of the ten dollars when I can."

There was a long silence during which a German cuckoo clock on the wall ticked away merrily. Then he said, "I'll write you out a bill of sale then, putting in what you've just said."

He wrote in beautiful copperplate script.

"You have beautiful handwriting," I said.

He smiled. "In my old country I was a clerk for a firm of lawyers. I used to write the briefs."

He finished the bill, then passed it to me to sign. I paid him the five dollars, thinking that there would be precious little left for food this week, and I could hardly ask Daniel for more in his current state. Then the man placed the locket in a little leather box and handed it with a solemn bow to Tig.

"I hope you soon have good news of your mother," he said.

"How do you think Uncle Jack got hold of Mummy's locket?" Tig asked as we made our way back home. "She never took it off."

I didn't like to share the thoughts that were crystallizing in my head. The worst of them was that Aunt Hettie and her man friend had killed Tig's mother and stolen her locket. Maybe they had killed her for her jewelry. People were certainly murdered for less in New York City. But for one locket? Tig's family had been poor. They had lived by the docks where his father worked. Apart from the locket, would she have had anything else worth killing for? Or perhaps she had interrupted some kind of criminal behavior, I thought. Overheard something she shouldn't.

I tried to think up some less frightening explanation to give to Tig. "I'm thinking that perhaps your mother left the locket behind when she went away, to make sure that Aunt Hettie took good care of you," I said.

"And when she didn't come back, Aunt Hettie thought she could keep the locket, right?" Tig asked.

"Maybe."

He turned away from me. "Then something bad has happened to her, hasn't it? We keep hoping and hoping that she will come back one day, but how can she be gone so long and not even write to us?"

"I'm afraid we may have to consider that possibility," I

said. "But we will find out the truth, Tig. It's always better to know than not to know."

He shook his head solemnly. I longed to put my arms around him and give him a big hug. He had endured so much worry and heartache for a little boy. I had just promised him that I'd find out the truth for him. Now I had to keep that promise somehow, although I had no idea how I was ever going to make it happen.

🍀 Fourteen 🍀

When I reached Patchin Place I found that Sid and Gus had returned home and taken Emmy to their house.

"Such a quiet little thing," Daniel's mother said, shaking her head. "It fair broke my heart watching her. Who would abandon a sweet child like that?"

"Nobody willingly," I said. "We're going to try and find out what happened to their mother."

I peeked in on Liam, who was playing happily with his blocks, then took Tig across the street to join his sister. Tig burst into the living room, where Emmy was sitting on the hearthrug, drawing. "Look, Emmy. Look what I've got."

He opened the box. Emmy's face lit up when she saw the locket. "It's Mummy's locket. It really is. Then she's close by, isn't she? She'll come for us any day now. Perhaps she was waiting for Christmas to surprise us."

I glanced across at Sid. Our eyes met but we remained silent.

"I think we should leave the locket here for safekeeping,"

I said to Tig. "You don't want to take it back to Aunt Hettie and risk losing it again."

"Very well." He handed me the box, with some hesitation.

"Miss Walcott and Miss Goldfarb will take really good care of it for you," I said. "And as soon as you are settled somewhere safe, you can have it back. You wouldn't want a big boy on the streets to take it from you, would you? Or Aunt Hettie's friend to pawn it again?"

"No." He shook his head emphatically.

"Why don't you children go into the kitchen and see what Gus is making for your lunch?" Sid said.

The worried look returned to Tig's face. "We should probably go back to our patch on the street," he said. "I don't think we can stay here."

"You are safe here, Tig," Sid said. "I promise you that you are safe. Miss Walcott and I care about you."

"I know," he said. "But Aunt Hettie expects us to bring home money every night."

"We can give you money to take home with you, if you really think you should go back there," Sid said. "But we've told you, you are welcome to stay here and sleep in a real bed and have a bath in a real big bathtub."

Tig nodded. "It's just that . . . what if Mummy did come back? How would she ever find us?"

"It sounds to me as if your Aunt Hettie might be glad to get rid of you, apart from the money you bring in," Sid said. "Maybe if Miss Walcott and I went to see your Aunt Hettie and told her we were taking you off her hands, she'd be pleased."

I could see that Tig was in an agony of indecision. Clearly he wanted to stay here, where he was warm and safe, but he couldn't extinguish the small hope that his mother would return.

"Don't worry about it now," Sid said. "Go into the kitchen with Emmy and have some cookies and milk."

As soon as they had gone Sid came over to me. "I went to the American Lines office," she said. "And I found their names. They came over in March. The names were Margaret Everett Jones, aged twenty-six, Thomas Montague Jones, aged eight, and Megan Everett Jones, aged four."

"That might explain the nickname Tig," I said. "Short for Montague."

"So was Everett her maiden name, do you think?" Sid asked.

"Her initials on the locket were *MEM*," I said.

"So Montague was probably her maiden name, then." Sid frowned. "That sounds more English than American. Upper-class English. Distinguished. I don't know how we are going to trace a family in England called Montague, do you?"

"When Daniel is better, he'll know how to contact the English police," I said. "And a name like Montague will certainly be easier to trace than one like Jones." I perched on the arm of the chair, holding out my hands to warm at the fire. I hadn't realized how cold I had become. "The big question is what an English aristocrat is doing here? Was there a family member she was hoping to meet?"

"A lover she was hoping to reunite with?" Sid suggested, coming to sit opposite me beside the fire.

"Or there's always the other possibility," I remarked as this idea formed in my head. "She wasn't coming here to look for someone. She was running away, trying to get away from something unpleasant in England."

"And the person she was running from found her and dealt with her?" Sid continued, "Or dragged her back to England against her will?"

"I have to think that Aunt Hettie is somehow involved in this," I said. "If she makes such a fuss about keeping the children, why doesn't she simply turn them out? And Tig said something interesting in the pawnshop. He recounted a conversation between Aunt Hettie and her male friend called Uncle Jack. When he told her to get rid of the kids, she replied that he knew why she couldn't do that yet. Tig took it to mean that their mother was returning to them. But I wonder if there was something more sinister or under-hand going on."

"She was being paid to keep them by someone else?"

"It's possible, isn't it?" I said.

"Then this is all part of a bigger plot." Sid stood up again. "Do you think we should confront Aunt Hettie? Have it out with her? Threaten to go to the police?"

"We have no proof of anything wrong," I said. "And I wouldn't want her to take it out on the children."

"We'll bring them here. If she tries to prevent that, we'll demand to know why."

I sighed, watching the flames of the fire lick upward at the chimney. "I'd be all for telling that woman what I thought of her," I said, "but my one reservation is that if their mother does return, Aunt Hettie might say she doesn't know where they have gone."

"Do you think their mother really might return after so long?" Sid asked. "What possible reason could there be for such a long delay with no communication whatsoever?"

I stood up suddenly. "What if there was communication? What if the mother has written to them regularly but Aunt Hettie destroyed the letters?"

"For what reason?"

"Money. What if she is blackmailing their family back in England saying she has the children, and will return them safely if she is paid?"

Sid shook her head. "None of this quite makes sense. If the mother can communicate with her children, she could also write to her family and tell them where the children are."

"But she might have run away from her family for some reason and have no wish to communicate with them."

Sid laughed suddenly. "Too complicated, Molly. No, I'm afraid the real explanation is quite simple. The mother has died. Aunt Hettie is keeping the children because they bring in a nice little sum of money every day, *and* because she suspects they might have good family connections and one day she'll be rewarded."

I stood up too. "I suppose you're right," I said. I turned to the mantelpiece as the pretty little ormolu clock chimed eleven.

"Eleven o'clock," I said. "Only an hour until I can go and visit Daniel. I've been worrying about him all night."

"He's in good hands at St. Vincent's," Sid said. "I'm sure it's just a matter of keeping the wound clean and letting it heal. At least they didn't have to cut him open and fish around for a bullet."

I nodded, unable to speak in case my voice betrayed my emotion. "I'd better go and get the children ready," I said at last. "I'm sure my mother-in-law will want to come with me to see Daniel, so we'll have to take the children."

"Leave them with us," Sid said.

"But you've already got Tig and Emmy."

"The more the merrier." Sid laughed. "And I'm sure Gus is making enough food for an army. She's convinced the children need fattening up and plans to do it in one day. Dumplings, I believe. And a suet pudding to follow. You and your mother-in-law are welcome to join us when you return."

"You're so kind." I smiled as I headed for the front door.

Daniel was sitting propped up in bed as we approached him. His eyes were closed and he still looked horribly pale. And so young, with a curl flopping boyishly across his forehead. My heart did a flip, thinking how close to death he had come, and how I couldn't bear to lose him. I found myself thinking of the other officer—the young one, new and keen in the department, the one who was carried out under a sheet, who didn't make it. Did he have a wife, a sweetheart, a mother, who was at this moment sitting staring hopelessly out of the window, wondering how she was ever going to go on without him? I had known when I married Daniel that danger and risk were part of his job, but it had never hit home until this year, when we were almost killed in a bomb explosion. And now this.

Daniel's mother took one look at him then rushed forward. "Oh, my dear boy," she said.

Daniel's eyes fluttered open. He looked around with surprise and then recognized his mother. "Hello, Ma," he said. "So you got here safely then? No holdup with the snow? That's good."

"Look at you," she said, taking his hand. "I've told you it was time to leave police work behind, haven't I? You've a wife and family now. What would have happened to them if you'd died? You need to move on to a safer job. For my sake. For Molly's sake."

Daniel looked past her and saw me standing at the foot of his bed. His face broke into a lovely smile. "I'm still here," he said. "And Molly understands. Don't you, my love?"

"His job is his life, Mother Sullivan," I said. "Did your husband abandon the police when you had a child?"

"No. He was as stubborn as his son," she said. "But I think all the worry and hardship brought him to an early grave."

"He was seventy-four, Ma," Daniel said with a chuckle. "That's hardly an early grave. Three score years and ten. That's the appointed life span, isn't it?"

"Don't say that," she snapped. "I'm seventy-two and I plan to keep going for a long while yet. What's more I want you to live out your full life—not to be stopped by a bullet."

"It was probably my fault," Daniel said. "I should never

have gone after the young idiot. I hoped to stop him in time. As if he could ever get to Antonio. There would be at least three rounds of bodyguards between him and the front door. All armed. All ready to shoot intruders. I hope he's learned his lesson."

"He's dead, Daniel," I said. "I saw them remove his body."

"Damn. He'd have been a good policeman, given time," Daniel said. He looked up at me again. "They didn't mean to shoot me, you know. We understand each other. I heard one of them shout in Italian something like, 'Not him, you fool. That's the captain,' right before a bullet knocked me over backward."

He looked around. "Where's my boy?" he asked. "Did you leave him with Bridie?"

"They don't allow children in the wards," I said. "He's with Sid and Gus at the moment."

"Is that wise?" He looked concerned.

"Of course. He loves being with them. And Bridie's with him."

"Let's hope they don't feed him curry or caviar or let him play with their knife collection," he said. He closed his eyes again as if talking had tired him.

"Did the doctor say how long you'll have to stay here?" I asked.

"A few more days," he said. "They want to make sure the wound doesn't turn septic. They are washing it with a disinfectant every couple of hours. Stings like hell."

"My poor darling." I smiled at him. "Still, you'll be home for Christmas and that's all that matters, isn't it?" I wanted to tell him about the English children. I wanted to ask him how to set about contacting people in England. And also how we'd find out whether their mother might have died. But I could see how weak he was. So I told him about Liam playing in the snow and the snowman we had started this morning and the goodies that his mother had brought with her. All positive things and no worries. The latter I kept to myself.

✖❂ Fifteen ❂✖

Tuesday, December 19

The next morning I opened the door to put out the milk bottles and jumped with alarm when something moved behind one of the box trees that grew in tubs on either side of Sid and Gus's front door. Then Tig stepped out of the shadows.

"For heaven's sake, Tig, what are you doing here?" I asked. "You nearly scared the daylights out of me."

"I'm sorry," he said as Emmy came to join him, "but we didn't want to wake you or the ladies too early. So we were waiting out of the wind for you to wake up."

"Come inside," I said, beckoning them to my front door. "We're letting the cold air in."

They didn't need much urging. The morning had a cold dampness that went straight to the bones. I saw then that they had a small bundle with them.

"Has something happened?" I asked.

Tig nodded as he pushed Emmy inside ahead of him. "We had to run away," he said.

I ushered them through to the kitchen, where Daniel's mother was busy making oatmeal on the stove.

"We have guests for breakfast," I said as I brought the two children into the warmth of the kitchen. "They've had to run away from the place where they were staying."

"Mercy me," my mother-in-law said. "What happened?"

Tig and Emmy stood shyly in the doorway. He glanced at her and then he said, "We heard them talking last night—Aunt Hettie and Uncle Jack. Her bedroom is right below the attic and we can hear a lot through the floorboards. He said, 'I told you you should have got rid of those brats ages ago. Now you'll find yourself in hot water if people come round here poking their noses in.'

"And she said, 'What was I supposed to do? I wanted to be paid, didn't I?'

"And he said, 'It's gone on long enough. Get rid of them.'

"And she said, 'Just turn them out, you mean? But that could be dangerous. They know some women who have been giving them clothes.'"

Tig paused, then looked up at me with big, frightened eyes. "And then Uncle Jack said, 'Get rid of them. We take them and throw them off the pier. They won't last two seconds in that frozen water. And then we say that they never came home one evening. Must have run away. Not your fault. No one can blame you.'"

Tig glanced at Emmy then looked back at us. "So I had to get Emmy away quickly, don't you see? They were going to throw us into the river. So we grabbed our things and came here, like you said."

"And you've been outside all night? You poor things."

Mrs. Sullivan poured hot tea into two cups. "Get that down you. It will warm you up. And the oatmeal should be ready any minute."

They sat at the table and sipped at the tea. It looked as if Sid and Gus had their wish to take in the children. I just hoped it didn't somehow backfire on them.

"So it sounds as if Aunt Hettie found out that you'd been to the ladies' house?" I said. "Do you think she was spying on you?"

"No, a boy told her," Tig said.

"Which boy?"

"A big boy. The one who makes me run errands for him. He was angry because I wasn't on my patch when he needed me so he found her and told her."

"Who is this boy?" I asked sharply. "And what does he have to do with you?"

"He's the one who said I'd taken that purse that time. He told me he'd give me a dime if I ran errands for him. I said no thank you, but he grabbed me by the shirtfront and he said, 'You don't want your little sister to get hurt, do you? I can protect her but only if you do what I say.'"

"And what were these errands, Tig?" I asked, feeling a sudden chill down my spine.

He looked sheepish now. "It was small packages, in an envelope or brown paper, tied up with string. He said I wasn't to open it if I knew what was good for me. But it felt like something—like a wallet—in there. I think it might have been wallets and purses that he stole. I wanted to say something, but I couldn't because of Emmy. I had to keep her safe."

"And where did you have to take these packages?"

"I had to take them to a place they call the Walla Walla," he said. "And give them to a man there."

"The Walla Walla?" I looked across at Daniel's mother. "That's the Walhalla Hall on Orchard Street where the Eastmans have their headquarters. That must mean that your boy is a Junior Eastman, and it proves to me that Daniel is quite right. The gangs have become involved in pickpocketing." I turned back to Tig. "But why didn't you tell me this before?"

Tig hung his head. "I was scared of what might happen to us. Those big boys—they are always around, watching us. Sometimes they take the money from the crossing sweepers."

"I understand," I said. "But don't worry. You're safe now. You won't need to go to that area again."

"Here you are," Mrs. Sullivan said. "Two bowls of oatmeal. You both look as if you need fattening up."

The children started eating. I poured myself some tea and helped myself to some oatmeal, joining them at the table. "Tig, I think we now know that someone was paying your Aunt Hettie to keep you. We just have to find out who and why. My husband is a policeman and he could question her, but he's in hospital at the moment, so we'll just have to be patient. Do you think Aunt Hettie knows where we live?"

He looked up worriedly. "I don't know. I don't think so."

"You'd better stay indoors, just to make sure. But the first thing to find out is why your mother brought you here. Do you ever remember a visit from her family when you were in England? Did she ever mention any of them?"

Tig frowned. "I don't think so. We had a visit once, long ago, from an American lady. I don't think Mummy was very pleased to see her. In fact she was quite upset."

"Was she a family member, do you think?"

He was still frowning. "I don't think so. The lady said she was on a tour of Europe, I remember that. Mummy was in bed sick. She was sick for a long time after she had Emmy. That's when we had to move and Daddy went to work on the docks."

"And your father's family? Did you never meet any of them?"

"I think he had some cousins in Wales, but I don't know where. His parents were dead. I don't think they ever came to visit us . . . and then Daddy died," he added with great sadness.

I remembered what Sid had told me. "Your middle name is Montague," I said. "Do you know why you're called that?"

"I don't know. Perhaps Mummy liked that name."

I felt frustration rising and had to remind myself that this was an eight-year-old child. Grown-ups tell them little, and most adult conversation goes over their heads. So it was possible that Montague had been their mother's maiden name. How could I possibly look into a Montague family in England? And what on earth had made her bring her children here—unless she had somehow been brought here against her will. I went over to the sink and let out my feelings of annoyance on the dirty oatmeal saucepan. It was awful to feel so powerless. But then it struck me that I did have something meaningful I could do here, if I could only find the time for it. When Daniel was safely out of hospital and at home again I could find out who was paying Aunt Hettie and whether Uncle Jack had anything to do with their mother's disappearance. Had he thrown her off a dock, the way he threatened to dispose of the children? And if so, why?

After the children had finished their breakfast I took them over to Sid and Gus, giving them a verbatim repeat of what Tig had told me. Gus, usually the sweet and more placid member of the pair, almost exploded with anger. "That dreadful woman. Calmly discussing killing two adorable children. We should go and tell her what we think of her. We should report her to the police."

Sid put a hand on her arm. "Calm down, dearest. We have to do what's best for the children, and right now we need to find out what happened to their mother. If we make an enemy of this witch we'll get nothing out of her. We have to pay her a visit and let her think we are doing her a favor by taking the children off her hands."

She looked at me for affirmation. I nodded. Gus sighed and wrapped a comforting arm around Emmy, who had been standing, wide-eyed, with her thumb in her mouth.

"Never mind," Gus said. "You are safe now and that's all that matters. I'm going to go up and light a fire in the back bedroom so that it's warm and cozy when you want to take a nap." She looked over the children's heads at me. "We had the beds already made up, thinking they were going to stay with us. I just wish I had some of my childhood toys with me. I had a lovely collection of dolls and horses and books."

Off she went up the stairs with an armful of newspapers

and firewood. Sid took Tig and Emmy through to the kitchen and set them at the table, ready to help her make gingerbread men. "We must get you some new clothes," she said as she helped Tig out of his jacket. "These are about to fall to pieces. I'll take your measurements and see what we can find at Macy's."

"We can't accept clothes from you, Miss Goldfarb," Tig said. "Mummy wouldn't like that. It's very kind of you to take us into your house and give us food."

"Don't be silly," Sid said. "We have plenty of money, Tig, and it will be fun for us to choose new outfits for you both. You can think of them as Christmas presents." She moved me away from the children into the hallway. "I think that you and I should pay a visit to this Aunt Hettie, don't you?" she whispered.

"Do we want her to know where the children are?" I whispered back. "What if they were being kept with her for some kind of criminal purpose? What if someone comes to harm them?"

"We'll make sure she doesn't see it as a threat, Molly. I'll tell her I saw the little girl on the street and took pity on her. I'll tell her it was very generous of her to keep them for so long when they could no longer pay for room and board, and I'm sure she's most grateful that I'm relieving her of that burden. I'll give her my card in case their mother turns up and mention that there will be a reward for help-ing to locate their mother."

I nodded. "Very smart, only I don't think I should come with you. I was already there, posing as a newly arrived Irish immigrant. She'll smell a rat if she sees me with you."

Sid nodded. "Very well. I'll go alone. It's better that way, and I'm absolutely sure that—"

She broke off as we heard the sound of Gus's boots coming down the stairs at a great pace.

"Molly, look at this!" Gus's voice echoed through the stairwell as she came rushing down the hallway toward us. She was waving a sheet of newspaper. "I was about to crumple this up to light the fire when the name caught my eye," she said. "It's yesterday's *Times*. The social column. Listen. It's your friend Miss Van Woekem."

She held up the newspaper and read, "'Miss Olivia Van Woekem, of Gramercy Park, for many decades a doyenne of New York society, is celebrating her eightieth birthday—'"

"How nice," I interrupted. "I should send her a card and go and visit her."

"Listen, there's more." Gus held up a hand to interrupt me. "'Is celebrating her eightieth birthday by announcing the engagement of her goddaughter Julia Hammond (only child of Harlan and Eliza Hammond, deceased) to Mr. Eustace Everett of Philadelphia.'"

"Everett," I exclaimed. "That's certainly a remarkable coincidence. How common would you say that name was?"

"Not very," Sid said.

"Then I should go and visit Miss Van Woekem today, to congratulate her on her birthday and the engagement of her goddaughter."

❈ Sixteen ❈

I knew enough of Miss Van Woekem to know that things had to be done properly at the correct time. I had been her companion when I first arrived in the city. We had started out as adversaries, but that had changed to mutual respect and even friendship. However, she was a lady of the old school. One could pay a call on her between eleven and twelve in the morning, or after three in the afternoon. Since I wanted to visit Daniel on the stroke of twelve, I would have to be patient and wait for the afternoon to visit her.

I went home, finished my morning chores, and then set off for St. Vincent's Hospital. Daniel's mother decided not to accompany me this time. "I'll stay here with the children," she said. "It's only right that Daniel has some time alone with his wife."

"If you're really sure," I said hesitantly.

"I know he's safe and on the mend, and I don't want you to feel that I'm here interfering in your lives."

"You know you are most welcome here. Liam loves his grandma and Bridie is thrilled to see you. And who else would bake us so many good things?"

She went slightly pink and I realized that perhaps the apprehension I always felt at her visits was mutual. Maybe she had sensed my hostility and had felt equally uncomfortable in my presence.

I put an arm around her shoulder. "I want you to enjoy your time here. We had planned to go and choose a Christmas tree, and I wanted to show you all the lovely decorated store windows. But I hadn't expected Daniel to get shot—" My voice cracked unexpectedly and she turned to give me an awkward hug.

"He'll be home with us before you know it," she said. "And we'll have a grand Christmas together."

I nodded and tried to smile, but frankly I felt quite overwhelmed at the moment. Christmas was turning out so differently from what I had hoped. I had said I didn't want to jinx things by saying that Daniel would be able to join us for dinner. Now he'd probably be lying in bed, an invalid, maybe unable to take part in any of the festivities. And now I also had a quest to find Tig and Emmy's mother. Maybe I would be able to put a piece into the puzzle this afternoon when I found out about Eustace Everett.

As the clocks around the city chimed noon I was going up the stairs to Daniel's ward. To my delight he was sitting up and already had some color back in his cheeks. His face lit up when he saw me. "Hello, my darling," he said. "Good of you to come."

"I'd have been here first thing this morning if the hospital didn't have such strict visiting hours," I said. "You're looking much better."

"My shoulder aches like billy-o," he said. "But I'm ready to go home as soon as they'll let me. The food here leaves a lot to be desired."

"Maybe if you tell the doctor that you have people to take care of you, and that you live close enough to check in with the hospital if anything goes wrong, they might let you come home," I said.

He nodded.

"Has anyone from the police department been to visit you?" I asked, and watched the shadow fall over his face.

"A sergeant pal of mine came in yesterday," he said. "It seems a rumor has been going around that the raid on the Italians was my idea—that I dragged the new kid along with me, and it was my fault he got shot."

"Daniel, that's terrible," I said. "Who could be spreading a rumor like that?"

"It probably comes straight down from the commissioner, or from Tammany," he said. "There are plenty who'd like to get rid of me. I'm a little too straight for some of them. I won't take bribes for one thing. And on the other hand, some of them think I'm too pally with the gangs. Which is rubbish. I'm not pally. I just know where to draw the line for my battles, and which battles I can never win."

"I hope your sergeant friend has found enough people on your side to set things straight. There must have been men at headquarters who saw you rushing after the new officer. Knowing you, I bet you yelled something like 'Where's that young idiot think he's going?'"

He smiled. "Probably. And it will all get straightened out in the end, I expect. But I'm tired of fighting—not just the crooks but my fellow officers. My father once said that he foresaw trouble when they made me a captain so young. He said there were toes I was treading on. And he was right. I was young and ambitious in those days, and I thought 'To hell with them.' But now I realize that grudges can be carried for years."

I took his hand, holding it in both of mine. "Oh, Daniel. I'm so sorry," I said. "And you are so good at what you do too. Such an asset to the police department."

"*Hmmph.*" He didn't answer that one.

"I can share one piece of information that may be interesting to you," I said. "Those beggar children we've taken under our wing—the boy told me he's been intimidated by an older lad and forced to run errands for him. It seems that the errands involve delivering a package to the Walhalla."

"The Walla Walla?" Daniel perked up and looked interested. "So the Eastmans are involved, huh? Did he say what was in the packages?"

"He didn't know. He was instructed not to open them. But he suspects it was purses and wallets stolen on the street."

"So I was right. The big gangs are taking over what used to be petty crime. That indicates to me that we're doing a good job at keeping major crime at bay, and the gangs are having to become opportunistic. Or it could be that Monk has had other things on his mind. He's being indicted for armed robbery and it looks as if they might finally be able to pin this one on him."

"He'll go to jail?"

"For a token amount of time, I expect, but the gang might take the opportunity to find a new leader. And it may be a case of 'While the cat's away the mice will play.'" He patted my hand. "Anyway, these matters don't concern you, Molly. I want my family to look forward to a grand Christmas together. Go ahead and buy the Christmas tree. Decorate the house. Make the cookies."

"I wanted you to be there to choose the Christmas tree," I said.

"We'll see what the doctor says." He closed his eyes as if talking had made him tired. "And, Molly." His eyes opened again, suddenly alert. "Don't get yourself involved in any way with these boys and the gang, understand. They may be young but some of them are vicious little thugs."

"Don't worry," I said. "This afternoon you'll be pleased to know that I'm doing something you'd quite approve of. I'm visiting Miss Van Woekem. It's her eightieth birthday."

"Well done," he said. "That's the spirit. Please give her my heartiest congratulations too."

As I left the hospital I went over what had been said—the lies spread about Daniel; the gang involvement in pickpocketing; and his clear delight that I was moving in the right social circles. There was something of his mother in him after all. I also realized that I had deliberately failed to mention my underlying reason for my social call. I didn't like deceiving my husband, but on this occasion it was better that he had nothing to upset him. And maybe today I could find out a little more about a family called Everett.

I came home and changed into one of my fancy gowns—rose-colored silk with pleating and tucking in the bodice and a spray of silk roses over the shoulder. It was never a dress I would have chosen for myself, but it had been pressed upon me by a wealthy woman, after my home was blown up, and I had accepted her offerings gratefully. And today it was proving a godsend, as I'd otherwise have had no dresses suitable for an afternoon social call in Gramercy Park. I pinned up my hair carefully, easing wayward curls into place, then put on my cape with the hood carefully adjusted over my hairstyle.

"My, don't you look elegant," my mother-in-law said as I came down the stairs.

"I have to pay a brief social call," I said. "An elderly friend is celebrating her eightieth birthday."

"An elderly friend? Clearly of the right social class, if you're dressed up like that."

"Miss Van Woekem," I said. Then my cheeks went pink. "Of course. You know her."

"We have met," she said. "You are starting to move in exalted circles, Molly."

I laughed nervously. "Not really. But I felt I should pay my respects on her eightieth birthday."

"Of course," she agreed.

"I hope you don't mind staying with the children a little longer."

"Not at all," she said. "I've no wish to go out when the

sidewalks are so treacherous. Take care yourself that you don't slip over."

"I will." I kissed her cheek.

I left Liam sleeping, Bridie knitting with some yarn that Daniel's mother had brought with her, and Sid and Gus busy making paper chains with Tig and Emmy. Then I set off. Snow flurries had picked up again and the sky was heavy with the promise of more snow. I toyed with the idea of taking a cab, but with Christmas coming and my husband sick in hospital, I couldn't sanction the additional expense. I had presumed the police department would take care of Daniel's hospital bills, but after what he had told me, I realized that I couldn't take that for granted.

So I walked down Waverly Place to Broadway and decided to brave the trolley instead. It wasn't that far up to Twentieth Street, but too far to walk on frozen sidewalks with snow blowing in my face. As I walked up Broadway to the nearest trolley stop I saw two boys, standing together in a doorway, watching shoppers pass them, rather like wolves examining a herd of deer. What's more, I recognized both of them. One was the boy who had recruited Tig to run his errands. The other was Malachy, Bridie's cousin. We had stayed with his family when we first arrived in New York and they had returned the favor by foisting themselves on me when they were thrown out of their apartment. The boys had always been trouble and I wasn't at all surprised that the older two had become Junior Eastmans.

Should I confront Malachy now, I wondered, but then I decided against it. I didn't want the other boy to find out where I lived and thus put my neighbors and Tig and Emmy in danger. Instead I decided to pay a call on Malachy's mother. She might be the most objectionable woman ever born, but she did have a sense of right and wrong, and still wielded some influence over her wayward sons. I didn't think she'd approve of picking pockets. Whether she could stop it was another matter, but at least I'd give it a try.

The trolley came along, its bell clanging. It was packed full, as usual, and I didn't think my silk dress would fare well from being jammed against so many bodies. It was only a short ride, but I was grateful to get off again at Twentieth Street. The windows of the stores on Broadway—Lord & Taylor and the other dry goods stores on this block— glittered with brightly lit snow scenes and enticing gift ideas. I realized I should bring a gift to Miss Van Woekem myself, so I went into Lord & Taylor and, having seen the prices, settled on a pair of embroidered handkerchiefs. Old ladies can never have enough handkerchiefs, I decided. I had them wrapped and then set off along Twentieth for Gramercy Park.

The gardens in the center of the square looked like a Christmas card scene, pristine behind their iron railings, untrodden, and with tree branches frosted with snow. Old memories came flooding back as I went up the steps to Miss Van Woekem's front door. The maid who answered it clearly did not recognize me as the drab peasant girl, newly arrived from Ireland, who had once worked there. I have to say that gave me a certain sense of satisfaction.

"Mrs. Molly Sullivan calling upon Miss Van Woekem," I said, and presented my calling card. "I trust she is at home."

"She is, madam. Please come in." The maid closed the front door behind me then took the card on a tray through to the front parlor. As she opened the door I heard voices. So Miss Van Woekem had other people to wish her well. I heard the conversation break off and then Miss Van Woekem's commanding voice saying, "Show her in, by all means."

My cape, scarf, and gloves were taken from me and I smoothed down my silk skirt before entering the room. Several women were sitting there, surrounding Miss Van Woekem, who occupied the big Queen Anne chair by the fire. She smiled and held out her hand to me. "Molly, my dear child. What a pleasant surprise."

"Forgive the intrusion," I said, going over to kiss her on the cheek, "but I saw the announcement of your birthday in the society column and felt that I had to stop by to give you my congratulations—on your birthday and the engagement of your goddaughter." I handed her my package. "And I brought you a small token."

She took it, smiling up at me. "How very kind. Do take a seat and join us. My maid was about to serve coffee and cake." She introduced me to the various women, none of whose names meant anything to me, but then I hardly ever read the society columns. I took a seat on an upright chair beside the sofa on which two middle-aged matrons sat. They nodded to me pleasantly.

"You live in Manhattan, do you, Mrs. Sullivan?"

"I do. Close to Washington Square."

"Washington Square? Really?" The larger of them raised

an eyebrow. "Is not that area overrun with students and immigrants these days?"

"And bohemians?" the other woman added. "One hears that artists and writers and the like are taking over that part of the city. We had a friend who had to move from Fifth Avenue because it was no longer a good address."

"I live on a little backwater and am not troubled by outsiders," I said, smiling sweetly.

Luckily at that moment a trolley was wheeled in, laden with various cakes and a coffee service. Coffee was served and the women beside me fell upon the cream cakes as if they hadn't had a decent meal in weeks. I couldn't help thinking that Tig and Emmy, who really were close to starving, had eaten more daintily.

"So tell me, do you know the bride-to-be?" one of the women asked me.

"I'm afraid I don't," I replied.

"Such a lovely girl. So tragic that her parents were both killed in the accident. Of course it has left her quite a wealthy woman, but one needs the guidance of a parent, doesn't one?"

"Miss Van Woekem has been a godsend to her. Having her to stay here while she introduced her to society."

I tried to keep my voice quite disinterested as I asked, "And the groom? What do you know of him? The name was not familiar to me."

"I haven't met him personally," one of them said, "but I understand that the Everetts are an old Philadelphia family."

"So he doesn't live in New York?"

"He does now, I believe. Is that not so, Miss Van Woekem?"

"What is that, Mrs. Farnham?" The old lady looked up at the summons. "Eustace Everett? Yes, he is now a dedicated New Yorker with a pied-à-terre at that monstrous Dakota building. But of course he spends a lot of time with his uncle out on Long Island, since he is now the heir and will take over the business when his uncle dies."

"Shipping, is it now?" one of the other ladies asked. "Imports?"

"That's right. Montague's Fine Java. They're tea and coffee importers. Mr. Montague's father made a fortune with the insatiable demand for coffee."

I had a mouthful of a rather crumbly cake and a crumb went down the wrong way. I rapidly put my napkin to my mouth as I coughed.

"The groom's uncle is Mr. Montague?" I asked when I was sure I could speak without spluttering.

"That's right. Such a lovely house in Great Neck on the Sound. Julia is so looking forward to hosting parties there in the summer."

"The young couple will live there then, will they?" one of the women sitting next to me asked.

"Some of the time. Of course when Mr. Montague dies they will inherit. And one understands that he is in the poorest of health. It can only be a matter of time."

"I'm sorry to hear that," one of the women mumbled.

"Tell me . . ." The large lady beside me leaned forward in her seat. Crumbs fell off an ample bosom. "Wasn't there some sort of tragedy or scandal with that family? Years ago?"

Various heads nodded. "Didn't the daughter run off with a servant?" The voice was lowered as if we might be overheard.

"Something like that. The music teacher, I believe— brought over here to give her singing lessons. Anyway, the father disinherited her. Cut her off completely and made Eustace his heir. Fortunately for your goddaughter, Miss Van Woekem."

The old lady smiled and I knew her well enough to read into her expression that she wasn't too fond of Mr. Eustace Everett.

I took my leave as soon as I dared without seeming rude, claiming that I had left my child with the nursemaid and he would need feeding. Miss Van Woekem took my hand, holding it in her cold and bony claw. "Come and see me more often, Molly, my dear. Bring the little one. Bring Daniel. I need young people around me, especially at this time of year."

"I will." I smiled into that sharp, birdlike face. "Daniel is currently in hospital, recovering from a gunshot wound, but as soon as he's up and around again we will most certainly be delighted to come and visit."

"Your husband is like a cat with nine lives," she said, eyeing me somberly. "And I believe he must have used up eight of them. Come to that, so have you. It's time you retired to the country and took up a less strenuous occupation. Let's talk about it when you visit next."

I smiled and nodded, then kissed her cheek and took my

leave. Was I being foolish ignoring so many warnings? Was it time we gave up a life tinged with danger and settled down to raise a family? But not just yet, I thought. I had finally found the missing piece of my puzzle. Margaret Everett Montague must have been the daughter who ran off with the music teacher and who had been cut off without a penny. And when her husband died and she could no longer cope with two children on her own, she had swallowed her pride and brought them back to America, hoping that her father would see the children and forgive her.

And then she had vanished. Or had she seen her father, been turned away once more, and killed herself in a fit of despair? Anyway, I knew where Eustace lived and I would have a chance to find out. And if the grandfather saw those adorable children, surely he would accept them and welcome them into his home. I felt a great bubble of optimism as I walked to the trolley stop.

✨ Seventeen ✨

Being of a rather impetuous nature I was tempted to go to the Dakota building right away and seek out Eustace Everett. But then I made myself see sense. He would probably be at work in his uncle's office, wherever that was. And when I approached him I would need proof—I'd take the locket with me for him to show to his uncle.

I arrived home to find Bridie over at Sid and Gus's house and the kitchen full of paper chains.

"As you can see we've started the preparations for Christmas," Gus called out merrily. "Sid is popping popcorn so that we can string it for the tree—which is very good of her, seeing that Christmas is actually not her holiday."

Sid looked up from the stove. "I'm happy to celebrate the spirit of Christmas because it brings peace and goodwill," she said. "And I'm all in favor of that. But the children shall also help me light the candles for each night of Hanukkah." A smile spread across her face as she looked at Gus. "What a treat for us to celebrate the season with children. I already feel that we have been given our holiday gift."

I swallowed back the news I was dying to share with them. It would not be fair to raise the children's hopes until I had something positive to tell them. So I waited until they were all three sitting threading popcorn and macaroni onto strings before I beckoned Sid and Gus out of the kitchen and told them the news. They were both excited.

"Montague's Fine Java. Of course we should have thought of that," Gus said. "We used to drink it back in Boston. So how will you proceed? Will you take the children to meet their grandfather or will you write to him first?"

"I was told that he's very ill and not expected to live long," I said. "I thought it would be more sensible to visit Eustace Everett first and show him the locket. Then he can take it to his uncle and give him the news at the right moment."

"Good idea," Sid said. She touched my arm. "Oh, Molly. I am so excited for the children. After what they have been through, to be reunited with a family who can provide for them well. It's such wonderful news."

"We mustn't jump to conclusions," I said. "Their grandfather cut their mother off without a penny because she married an unsuitable man. We can tell from what the children remember that their father was a loving and kind man and that their mother was happy with him. So the grandfather is clearly an inflexible and uncaring type. He may not welcome his grandchildren even now."

"How could he not welcome two such adorable children?" Gus said. "Surely they would melt the hardest of hearts?"

"I hope so," I said. "I'll pay a visit to Eustace Everett tomorrow morning if I can."

"And I will pluck up courage and pay a call on wicked Aunt Hettie this afternoon," Sid said. "I should tell her what we plan to do before nightfall so that she knows the children are safe."

"Not that she'd care," Gus said indignantly.

"But we don't want her to notify the wrong people either," I said.

"Wrong people?" Gus asked.

"Someone, somewhere is clearly paying her to keep the children," I said. "Otherwise, with an unfeeling nature like hers she would have turned them out long ago."

"Perhaps their mother left enough money for their room and board and Aunt Hettie is keeping most of it and making the children sleep in the attic. But she's not turning them out completely in case the mother returns," Gus suggested.

I shook my head. "There's more to it than that, Gus," I said. "I'm still not sure we're doing the right thing by telling Aunt Hettie where the children are."

"Would you have me send them back to her? Have them living in constant fear of when they might be thrown into the river, Molly?" Sid demanded.

"Of course not. I'd prefer to have her worry about where they might have gone and who they might have told about the way she treated them. It would serve her right to live with that worry and uncertainty."

"But you do see that their mother would need to know where to find them, on the off chance that she returns to them," Gus said.

I sighed, glancing down the hallway to make sure that little ears were not listening. "I think we have to assume that a tragedy has befallen their mother. I suspect she might have been to see her father, who rejected her yet again, thus causing her to end her own life in despair."

"Let us then hope that the children melt their grandfather's heart of stone and are reunited with him before he dies," Gus said.

Amen to that, I thought.

I took Bridie home with me to find my mother-in-law had dinner on the stove and Liam sitting happily in his chair, thoroughly sticky with a slice of bread and jam.

"Well, here you all are," she said, smiling at us. "So tell me about your afternoon excitements." I could never tell from her expression whether she was annoyed, or felt that she was being taken advantage of, at being left home alone with Liam. Those things would only come out later when she'd casually mention them to Daniel. But perhaps I was misjudging her. Perhaps she was happy to be part of the family and to take care of us all.

"We made paper chains and then we strung popcorn for the tree," Bridie said. "And Miss Walcott made gingerbread men and they were so good."

Daniel's mother nodded, trying to find it in her heart to approve of the actions of my neighbors of whom she so heartily disapproved. "And how was Miss Van Woeken?" she asked. "Is she well?"

"She looks very frail, but she has looked that way since I first met her," I said.

"I forget now—when did you meet her?"

"Soon after I arrived in New York." I went to pour myself a cup of tea.

"And how did your paths cross? I wouldn't have thought you moved in the same social circles in those days."

I smiled. "I was her companion. I had to push her around the park and read to her. Our relationship was quite thorny at first, but we came to respect each other and now I'm actually rather fond of her."

"But you didn't stay long as her companion?"

"No, I couldn't stay any longer after I discovered—" I broke off what I had been going to say. After I discovered Daniel had deceived me and was engaged to another woman. And that other woman was another goddaughter of Miss Van Woekem. Painful memories flashed through my mind. "I decided I was not cut out to be a servant," I said. "I was more suited to running my own business. I wasn't born to be humble." And I managed a bright smile.

"When are we going to get a Christmas tree?" Bridie asked.

"Daniel said that we should go out and choose one before the good ones are gone," I replied, "but I'd much rather wait until he's home and can come with us."

"He may not be up to walking around much for a while," Mrs. Sullivan said. "And he certainly shouldn't be jostled by crowds. It could open the wound again."

"You're right," I said. "Then it's decided, Bridie. We'll all go to choose the tree tomorrow. But we'll wait to decorate it until Captain Sullivan is home with us."

"Do we have any indication when that might be?" Daniel's mother asked.

"In the next few days, he seemed to think. He was looking so much better already."

"He'll be home for Christmas. That's all that matters," she said.

She went across to the shelf and took down a cardboard box. "I'm not sure whether you have any ornaments, after your fire this year," she said. "So I've brought down Daniel's favorites from when he was a little boy."

She started to unpack them from tissue paper, one by one: bright glass balls of various sizes, a blue glass bird with a feather tail, a tiny glass trumpet, a glass acorn, a bunch of grapes. Then a star to put on top of the tree, and candleholders for the branches.

"They are lovely," I said. "I was wondering today what we'd use to decorate the tree, and here you've provided everything we need once again."

"And don't forget my popcorn chain," Bridie said.

"Of course not. No tree would be complete without chains. And we should decorate some walnuts to hang on the branches. And maybe some small apples."

Bridie nodded with satisfaction. "It's going to be the best tree ever," she said.

We were just sitting down to dinner when there was a knock at the front door. I went to open it and found Sid standing there.

"I did it, Molly," she said. "I went to see her—the old witch."

"And?" I asked.

"She was quite as horrible as you describe. The most unpleasant woman I've ever encountered. Interested only in money, I came to realize. I told her that we had seen the children begging and decided to do the charitable thing by taking them off the streets until the weather gets warmer. I asked if she had any idea what might have happened to their mother so we could help locate her. She claimed she had no idea. Walked out and left the children and never came back. That's all she knew. I said that of course I realized she had a business to run and couldn't be responsible for someone else's children. So we'd obviously be doing her a favor by taking them off her hands, and if she did hear anything that might lead us to their mother, of course there would be a reward."

She looked at me angrily. "You should have seen her eyes light up at the word 'reward.' Until then I could tell she was ambivalent, not sure if she was being tricked into something, or accused of not treating the children properly. But then she was all smiles and said she'd be sorry to lose the little dears, but of course she didn't have the time or space to care for them like we could. 'Please give the little dears my fondest wishes,' she concluded."

"You handled it very well, Sid," I said. "Won't you come in?"

"No, I need to be there to assist Gus with bath and bed." She smiled. "This is quite a new experience for us—to be instant parents. I rather like it so far."

I watched her as she hurried back across the street.

Parenting was a novelty to them—their latest fad. But what would happen if we did not reunite the children with their family? If they realized they were to be stuck with two children for the long term? I pushed aside that worrying thought as I closed the front door.

꧁ Eighteen ꧂

We spent the evening talking about Christmas
preparations. Bridie was determined to knit
Emmy a new scarf, even though she wouldn't
have to be out in the cold anymore. Daniel's mother was
also busy with her knitting, finishing up a jacket for Liam.
Never having been the world's best knitter, I felt inadequate.
I realized Daniel and I had talked about Liam's Christmas
present, and also a surprise for Bridie, but as yet I had nothing for Daniel, his mother, or Sid and Gus. I had expected
to have ample time to think about these things, not to be
embroiled in yet more worries.

On Wednesday morning I bundled up the children and
we all went together to the Jefferson Market, which was in
full early morning swing. Piles of vegetables on stalls all
around. The earthy aroma of potatoes mingling with the
strong smell of Brussels sprouts, and among them sprigs
of holly, of mistletoe. Then the occasional flash of color,
mounds of squash and pumpkins, a display of oranges, some
of them wrapped in foil, ready to be stocking gifts.

We smelled the Christmas trees before we found

them—that delicious fresh piney smell. And there they were—spruce fresh from New England and Upstate New York. Bridie gave an excited little squeal and darted forward. "They are so beautiful," she exclaimed.

We stood back and let her choose, smiling at each other when she chose modestly, not the biggest tree, but one that she could lift herself. We also bought nuts and butternut squash to roast, a pumpkin to make into soup, and a sprig of holly. Bridie insisted on carrying the tree home herself. Once home, we put it in a bucket of water outside the back door so that it would still be quite fresh when Daniel came home.

Bridie asked to let Tig and Emmy see our tree and went over to fetch them. When they came back, I showed the children how to make paper snowflakes and left them sitting deep in concentration at the table. Then I decided I had enough time to slip away before visiting hours at St. Vincent's Hospital.

"Would you mind if I went out for a few minutes?" I asked my mother-in-law. "We've been trying to locate the children's family and I think we might finally have a lead."

"Really? But aren't they English?" Mrs. Sullivan asked me. "Do they have family over here?"

"They came over from London, to be sure," I said, "but I now think that their mother was American and she brought them back here after their father died, hoping to be reunited with her family here. Does the name Montague mean anything to do?"

She thought for a minute, then shook her head. "There is no Montague I can think of in Westchester County, and

I've no real knowledge of society within the city these days." She looked up at me. "But you go and do what you can. The children are happily occupied and the little fellow just likes being with them."

I kissed her cheek. "You are very kind to us and I do appreciate it. I'm glad you're part of our family at Christmas."

She looked rather embarrassed and pleased, and I realized that she must be lonely in that big house in Westchester County and glad to be with us. I took the locket in its little leather box, put it in my purse, then I bundled up and went out into the snowy streets, catching the Sixth Avenue El to the Upper West Side. It was this train that had almost killed me and my son and I still had qualms about boarding it, but I told myself not to be so silly. Accidents happen and one accident was not going to spoil the rest of my life. All the same, I found I was holding my breath as the train rounded the sharp curve to join the tracks of the Ninth Avenue train.

We arrived without incident and I descended at the Sixty-sixth Street station, heading toward the park. The sun came out between clouds as I approached the park and it gleamed and sparkled like a winter wonderland. Even though I was in a hurry and had a task to complete I couldn't help going up to the railings, watching the bright figures skating on the lake and small boys dragging sleds behind them. A perfect scene for the Christmas season, I thought.

Then I turned to that magnificently monstrous edifice, the Dakota building. It was the first luxury apartment block built so far north, away from the center of town and at the edge of the park. Hence the name—so far west that it was almost in the Dakotas. Now the city had spread north and west to join it, with other such apartment buildings rising in majestic splendor on this side of the park, while the East Side now boasted its museums and mansions. I went up to the imposing front entrance, where a doorman in full livery greeted me, and asked for Mr. Eustace Everett's residence.

He frowned. "I'm afraid Mr. Everett is not here at the moment, ma'am. He went out early this morning and I suspect you will find him at his place of business."

"Montague Coffee Importers?" I asked. "Would you happen to know where that is?"

"On Wall Street, so I am given to understand, ma'am. Down toward the docks."

I thanked him and set off again with a sigh. Having come so far north to now head to the southern tip of Manhattan was most frustrating. I told myself that the children were in good hands and the Sixth Avenue El would take me down to South Ferry, from where it would only be a short walk to Wall Street. So I made my way back to the station and found that my heart no longer pounded quite so violently as the train rounded the curve where the accident had taken place. An icy wind was blowing off the Atlantic when I climbed down the steps to the street below and the usually placid meeting of the Hudson and East Rivers was flecked with whitecaps as well as floating ice. A most unappetizing scene, I shivered as I pictured Tig and Emmy being thrown into such water. Only a monster would consider such a deed, I thought, and picked up my pace toward Wall Street. I was so glad they were safely with Sid and Gus.

There was no mistaking the Montague Coffee Importers building. It was at the very end of Wall Street, facing the docks, and the aroma of coffee betrayed its presence before I saw the name painted across the brickwork. The open doors to the warehouse showed an expanse piled high with sacks of coffee. Laborers were hoisting sacks onto their shoulders and then carrying them off and up a flight of stairs, bending and staggering under the weight. I walked past until I found a separate entrance and went up a flight of narrow stairs to a dark hallway. I didn't think this could be the right place to find the owner's quarters, but at least I'd find somebody who could direct me. As I was looking around a young clerk emerged from a side cubicle. He was a lanky youth with red hair brighter than my own. "Can I help you, ma'am?" he asked.

I asked if Mr. Everett was available.

"He is, ma'am. But he's very busy today. We've a ship just docked from Brazil. Would our foreman, Mr. Grimes, or Mr. Everett's secretary do instead?"

"No, I wish to speak with Mr. Everett himself," I said. "It will not take long."

"May I ask what this is about?"

"A personal matter of great urgency. One concerning his family," I said.

"Please wait here, I will inquire whether he will see you." He looked downright scared as he headed into darkness along the hall. I waited. There was nowhere to sit, but at least it was warm and smelled of coffee. At last he returned. "Mr. Everett had agreed to give you a couple of minutes of his time, if you will follow me."

He set off at a great rate, while I followed. Along the

hall and up another flight of stairs. Then he tapped on a door and I was ushered into a bright, well-appointed office. After the Spartan conditions of the stairs and hallway I was surprised by the thick carpet, mahogany bookshelves, and desk. The view from the window looked out over the East River, where, in spite of the cold conditions, there was a hive of activity. Small figures unloaded crates and pushed barrows. Their shouts and cries echoed up to us. Directly in the foreground a sailing ship was being eased into a berth. It was interesting to note that there was a distinct absence of steamships to be seen. I tried to imagine those small vessels negotiating the Atlantic in conditions like today's.

All this flashed through my mind in an instant before the man at the desk swiveled around in his chair to face me. He was young, a trifle on the podgy side, with neatly parted dark hair, round cheeks, and fleshy lips. Not unattractive, but somehow with a spoiled look to him. Clearly one who was used to privilege.

"Ah—Eustace Everett. And you are?" he asked. He spoke in a clipped manner and I noticed he did not smile or offer me a seat.

"Mrs. Sullivan," I said, "and I am sorry to disturb you when I understand you are so busy."

"What's this about?"

"It's about your cousin, Margaret Montague," I said.

This really surprised him. His eyebrows shot up. "Margaret? She's been gone for years. Don't tell me she's come back?"

"I believe she did return to New York a few months ago," I said. "So she did not try to contact you or her father?"

"She certainly didn't try to contact me," he said. "She may have tried her father, but she'd have been out of luck. I don't know how much you are aware of our story, Mrs. Sullivan, but Margaret was foolish enough to run off with a servant . . ."

"The music teacher, I believe."

"Whatever he was, he was not of her social standing. A penniless man of the lower classes and not a suitable match in any way. When her father found out that they had eloped he made it quite clear that she was no longer his daughter. He cut her out of his will and said she was never to be spoken of again." He looked up at me suddenly. "My uncle is a hard man, Mrs. Sullivan. If Margaret had returned and begged to see him, his pride would not have allowed it. Besides, he is in poor health at the moment."

"So I understand," I said. "I am very sorry."

His eyes narrowed. "So may I ask the reason for your visit today? Is it possible you have been sent as an emissary from my cousin?"

"No. I have never met your cousin," I said. "But I have met her children. I found them begging on New York streets and when I heard their story I resolved to help them."

"May one ask where my cousin is if her children are reduced to begging?"

"I wish I knew. All I can tell you is that she brought them to New York, left them in the care of a woman who runs a boardinghouse, and then disappeared. That was in March and nothing has been heard of her since. So one has to assume that some kind of tragedy has befallen her."

"You heard this story from whom exactly?"

"The children," I replied.

He gave me a supercilious smirk. "I'm not sure what to think about this—whether the children put you up to it, or you saw the children as a good opportunity."

"Are you suggesting that I am helping the children for my own gain, Mr. Everett? Really, you must be a poor judge of character." I fought to keep my temper. No sense in walking out and making him an enemy when he was the one person who might be able to help us.

That supercilious smile still lingered at the corners of his lips. "Then maybe you are a kindhearted woman of the sort who does good deeds among the poor in the city. Well meaning, but naïve. These children told you they were Margaret Montague's offspring, did they? My dear Mrs. Sullivan—the news of my engagement was just in the newspapers. Such mentions bring people like you out of the woodwork. Hitherto unknown relations, people who claim I owe them money . . ." He paused, took out a big handkerchief, and blew his nose.

I waited. He put the handkerchief away, then said, "Do you have any proof at all that these are my cousin's children? The children know of their mother's family and heritage?"

"They knew very little, Mr. Everett. Apparently she never spoke of her family. But we have seen the ship's manifest and their names were clear enough to be proof. Margaret Everett Jones and her children, Thomas Montague Jones and Megan Everett Jones. What more proof do you need?"

When he didn't answer I said, "Might I bring the children to see you? I'm told the little one strongly resembles her mother."

"I hardly knew my cousin, Mrs. Sullivan," he replied. "I grew up in Philadelphia and was only brought to New York after Margaret ran off and her brother was killed, and it was realized that I was now the heir. And the Montague family can be thankful for that. Margaret was a female and thus not equipped to run a business of this scope and magnitude, and David would never have buckled down to work as I have. He liked his pleasures and took nothing seriously, from what I've been told."

"How did he die?" I asked.

"A riding accident. He tried to show off and jump a particularly tall gate. He was thrown and broke his neck."

"Your poor uncle," I said. "And how fortunate that you were able to come and take the place of his children."

He gave a satisfied little nod, apparently not realizing the element of sarcasm in my remark. "Yes, it has been fortunate, for him and for me."

"And soon you are to be married. My congratulations."

"Thank you. I am well satisfied. It is a good match. But if you'll excuse me, I must return to work. I'm afraid there would be no point in my meeting your beggar children. I have only the dimmest memory of my cousin, and I certainly couldn't upset my uncle with this kind of outrageous news. In his precarious current state of health it might even kill him."

He swiveled his chair around, indicating I was dismissed and he wanted to get back to work.

"You asked if I had proof, Mr. Everett," I said. "Actually

I do." He stopped and then turned his chair back toward me. I reached into my purse and brought out the leather box, placed it on his desk, and then opened it. "This is the locket their mother always wore. It bears her initials and inside are two locks of hair—one is hers and the other her brother's. If you would show that to your uncle, I'm sure he would agree to see the children."

He took it and examined it, holding it in his podgy hands.

I went on, more boldly now, "Surely if these are your cousin's children, your own flesh and blood, you would not want them to freeze to death on the streets of New York? And is it not possible that your uncle would want to know he has grandchildren? All I ask is that you show this to your uncle at the right moment. If he still refuses to acknowledge them, then so be it. But I can't believe he would turn them away."

He took the locket and replaced it in the box. "Very well, Mrs. Sullivan. I will do as you ask. As it happens I'm to go out to Oyster Bay tomorrow with my fiancée to make sure everything is in order for our big engagement party on Saturday. If my uncle seems well enough I will show it to him."

"Thank you. I am most grateful," I said. "They are lovely little children and deserve something better than the New York streets." I reached into my purse. "Here is my card," I said. "Please send me a note as soon as you have news."

"Of course. Now I really must get back to work."

He was already examining a sheaf of papers as I left the room. There was no sign of the young clerk and I found my own way back to the street.

❦ Nineteen ❦

I just had time to go home to check on the children before
it was visiting hours at St. Vincent's Hospital. This time
I bundled up Liam and Bridie, hoping that Daniel might
be well enough to look out of the window and see his son.
Daniel's mother came with us too. Liam was keen to be out
of the buggy and playing in the snow, leaning forward in
his harness, holding up his arms, and making urgent cries.

"Hush your noise. You can't get out now. We're going
to see Dada," I scolded. He was such an adventurous little
soul that I wanted to keep him safely contained for as long
as possible.

When we reached the hospital I sent my mother-in-law
up first. It was only right after she had been kind enough to
watch the children for me the last time I visited. I wheeled
the buggy around to where I thought Daniel's window
should be and told Liam to watch. Any minute now Dada
would appear. Then a face came to the window—not Daniel's but his mother's. She was beckoning to me urgently. A
wave of fear shot through me. Something had happened to
Daniel. He had had a relapse during the night. Gangrene

had set in, or infection. Hurriedly I pushed the buggy around to the entrance. I couldn't take it up the steps and was wondering what to do next when my mother-in-law herself appeared, breathing heavily as if she had run part of the way.

"What is it? Bad news?" I asked as she came down to us.

"No, good. They say he's ready to go home. He's all dressed and waiting."

"Why, that's splendid. Couldn't be better." I hugged her.

"So why don't I wheel the buggy back with the children and you can bring him home in a cab," she said.

"Yes. Perfect." I was so relieved I was almost lost for words. "That's very kind of you," I managed to stammer.

"Not at all, my dear. You go up to your husband now."

I watched them walk away with Bridie helping to push the buggy, then I bounded up the stairs to Daniel's ward. He was sitting on a chair beside his bed, dressed in a jacket I didn't recognize. He still looked horribly pale, but he broke into a big smile when he saw me.

"Good news, eh, Molly? They say the wound is healing nicely and as long as we wash and dress it twice a day and I try not to move too much, I should be right as rain in a few days."

"That is good news." I bent to kiss him. "So are you ready to go home? I'm sure you're not allowed to walk yet."

"When I'm ready they will take me down in a wheelchair to the casualty entrance," he said. "So perhaps you can go and hail a hansom cab?"

"I will," I said. I beckoned to a young sister. "Captain Sullivan is ready to leave," I said. "Should I go and find a cab for us now?"

"You should, Mrs. Sullivan. And we'll meet you around the side, where they bring in the ambulances."

"Will my husband be warm enough dressed like that?" I looked at him critically. "And where did that jacket come from?"

The sister laughed. "From the poor box, I'm afraid. It was the only one in his size. His own clothes were so blood-stained they had to be thrown away. But we'll wrap him in a blanket. You can return it to us when you can."

"Thank you." I smiled at her. "I'll see you downstairs then, Daniel."

And off I went. Soon a hansom cab was found, Daniel was helped up to the seat, the driver was instructed to drive slowly and avoid the bumps if he could, and we started for home. Even moving at a sedate pace it was still a bumpy ride over lumps of snow and ice in the street, and I glanced nervously at Daniel each time the cab lurched. But he returned my worried glances with a smile. When we came to Patchin Place the cabby was unwilling to take the vehicle up such a narrow street, knowing that he'd not be able to turn it around and not wanting to back up the horse.

I persuaded him to go at least halfway, then asked him to help Daniel descend. I gave him a generous tip then made Daniel take my arm as I led him to the house. Bridie and Liam had made it home first. They had been waiting with anticipation, watching out of the parlor window, and rushed to greet him. I had to fend them off. "Carefully now, Liam," I said as he hurled himself at his father. "Dada hasn't been well. We have to treat him gently."

"It's good to see you, my boy." Daniel ruffled Liam's dark

curls. "And your dada will be right as rain and ready to play with you again very soon." He stood there with a contented smile on his face. "It smells wonderful in here," he said.

"Well, we've been baking," I said. "Would you like to go straight up to bed or should I make you comfortable in the parlor?"

"I'd like to sit in the kitchen and have something to eat with my family," he said. "I've been doing too much resting recently."

"Your mother has made an Irish stew," I said. "We were going to have it tonight, but I expect you'd like some now."

Daniel's eyes lit up. Irish stew was one of his favorites. He made it down the hallway under his own steam. I helped him to sit at the table and I served the stew. Daniel ate with relish. "Ma, you've outdone yourself this time," he said. "Nothing ever tasted so good, especially after that hospital food. If you don't die from your wounds there, the food will kill you pretty soon."

"Is it poisoned?" Bridie asked, looking worried.

"Captain Sullivan is just making a joke, my darling," I said. "He just means that the food isn't as tasty as his mother makes."

"Don't worry, son, I'll soon get your strength back for you," Daniel's mother said. "Plenty of good soups and pies and puddings. That's what you need."

"And we made gingerbread men and all sorts of good things," Bridie said. "And we made lots of paper snowflakes." She got up to show Daniel. "We're going to hang them in the windows."

"My, you were busy," Daniel said.

"Tig and Emmy made them too," Bridie said.

"Tig and Emmy?"

"The children we found on the street," I said.

"You've been bringing them here?" He frowned.

"No, they live with the ladies across the street now," Bridie said.

"What?" Daniel looked up angrily. "Another impetuous act they may well come to regret, I fear. Didn't I warn you about street children?"

"Hold your horses, Daniel. Sid and Gus have taken them in after the children heard their landlady and her man friend debating whether to get rid of them by throwing them off one of the Hudson piers," I said.

"Good God." Daniel looked stunned.

I was about to ask him whether he knew anything about a Jack Hobbs but swallowed back the words, reminding myself that he had just come out of hospital. "But we shouldn't worry you with any of this right now, Daniel," I said. "The children are safe at the moment and we may have located their family. So all will be well."

"Well done. How did you trace their family?" he asked.

"It's a long story." I didn't want to raise Bridie's hopes before all was settled.

"I think I had better go and sit somewhere more comfortable," Daniel said, pushing his plate away from him. "This shoulder is beginning to ache again."

"Would you like to take a nap?" I asked. "I'll help you get undressed upstairs."

"No, I'd rather stay up. It's easier on the shoulder to sit," he said. "And I should start moving around to get my strength back." He started walking, somewhat unsteadily, down the hall. I followed, ready to catch him if he stumbled. He stood in the parlor doorway, looking at the sofa and the armchair by the fire, then settled on the sofa. I grabbed all the pillows and propped him up. Then I found the afghan and tucked that over him.

"How's that?" I asked.

He smiled up at me. "You're gentler than the nurses at that hospital. They tossed me around as if I was a sack of potatoes."

"I'll be back after I put Liam down for his nap," I said.

I scooped up the protesting Liam and carried him upstairs. Bridie came too and I left her singing him his favorite nursery rhymes. I returned to Daniel. "That girl is a godsend," I said. "She can quieten Liam better than I can." I added coal to the fire before I sat beside him.

"So what is the long story about these street children?" he asked.

I told him about my locating Eustace Everett and my visit to him, then added, "But we are still trying to find out what happened to their mother. She brought the children from England after their father died, obviously hoping to reunite with her father. She left the children saying she would return shortly and never came back. If you were well and at work, I'd ask you to look through police records and see if any young woman matching her description was found dead at the end of March."

"You have a description, do you?" he asked.

"I'm told her daughter looks just like her, so I could describe her quite well."

"It should be easy enough to check the records," Daniel said. "I'll send a message to one of my constables and have him do it. If you bring me pen and paper, you can hand it in at the Jefferson Market station, and someone there will see it's delivered."

"Thank you, Daniel." I beamed at him and went to his desk to bring him paper, pen, and ink.

"What makes you think she's dead?" he asked.

"Something must have happened to her. She would never have abandoned her children."

"Some women do, out of desperation."

I shook my head. "The children clearly adored her. She would only do such a thing if she was of unsound mind—"

I broke off in the middle of what I had been going to say. Of unsound mind. Of course, I had never considered that before. Tig had told me that his mother had been ill since the birth of Emmy. Was it possible she had had a mental collapse? That the strain of losing her husband and bringing the children to America had brought it on again? Was she at this moment locked away in an insane asylum or even wandering the streets, not remembering who she was?

"It's just possible that she might have had some sort of brainstorm and lost her reason," I said. "The boy told me his mother had been sick for a long time after she gave birth to the little girl. It's possible that was some kind of mental illness. It does happen after the birth of a child, so I've heard."

Daniel nodded. "Then she could be anywhere."

"You could ask your man to check the records at the insane asylum on Ward's Island. I could go and check it myself, but—"

"Oh, no," Daniel said firmly. "I'm not letting you anywhere near that place again. I remember what almost happened to you the last time."

"That was because I was posing as an inmate," I said.

Daniel sighed and shook his head. "It's a wonder you ever survived to marry me and have Liam," he said. His hand reached out to cover mine. "But now that I have you, I'm not about to lose you again. Nothing dangerous, Molly. Promise me."

"I promise. This is a simple case of a missing person, Daniel. We have her name. We have a description. If something has happened to her in New York, then surely your men can find out for me."

Daniel wrote for a while then put the letter into an envelope. "I'm sending this to Constable Byrne. He's always been a good sort and looks up to me."

"He was the one who came to tell me you'd been shot," I said. "He took it upon himself to leave what he was supposed to be doing and run to find me."

"Yes, that's the sort of thing he would do. I've asked him to come round here first thing tomorrow morning, and you can give him the description and details yourself. That way there is no risk of anything being intercepted at headquarters."

I had been looking into the fire, watching the flames dance upward. Now I looked up in surprise. "Are you implying that your mail might be opened and read at your headquarters?"

Daniel shrugged. "Who knows? If there really is a conspiracy to get rid of me, then someone might well want to take a peek at a letter sent from me."

"That's disgusting, Daniel. And you think this all comes straight from the commissioner?"

"Either him or his cronies at Tammany. Either way, I'm not taking any chances."

I picked up the letter. "I'll go now and drop this off at the Jefferson police station." I went to the hallstand to put on my cape and scarf. "I'll only be a minute," I called, and off I went.

It was bitterly cold with the promise of even more snow, and my cheeks stung in the wind. I handed in my letter, and as I slithered my way home snowflakes were already floating downward. Daniel's mother was already sitting beside him, her knitting in her lap, when I returned. I went to make myself busy in the kitchen, still concerned about what Daniel had told me. Daniel had loved his job. He had devoted his life to the New York police department as had his father before him. It was horrible to think that there was now a faction working to oust him, and that presumably he didn't know who was on his side and whom to trust.

I had just put in some scones to bake for tea when there was a thunderous knock on our front door. I wiped my hands on my apron as I went to open it. I was expecting to see Gus, Sid, or one of the children, but instead it was Constable Byrne himself, his cheeks bright red from the cold.

"Constable Byrne, how good of you to come so quickly," I said. "Do come in, and let me pour you a cup of coffee or tea. It's freezing out there."

"It surely is, Mrs. Sullivan," he replied. "I take it the captain is home, then, if he wrote a letter with this address."

"He is. We brought him home this afternoon. Come on through. He's in the parlor."

The constable wiped his feet carefully and brushed the snowflakes from his jacket before he followed me into the room.

"Constable Byrne," I heard Daniel say warmly. "How good of you to come."

"Anything for you, Captain. So good to see you up and around again. When I saw you lying there on Mulberry Street I felt for sure you were a goner."

"I was damned lucky," Daniel said. "The bullet went right through and out the other side without touching any vital organ. But I understand that Sparks was not so lucky."

"Killed outright, poor beggar. And you know what they are saying at headquarters? They are saying that you sent him to arrest Antonio Spagnelli."

"So Sergeant Halloran told me," Daniel said. "I hope you helped put them straight."

"I and several others told them there was no way the captain would do that. In fact the constable at the front desk said he'd heard you shouting angrily when someone told you where Sparks had gone, and that you'd rushed after him. But once a rumor gets started there are always going to be some who believe it. So there's bad feeling, especially because they're saying you let Sparks take the bullet."

"Damn their eyes," Daniel muttered. "I can't wait to get back there and set them straight. And I bet I know who started the rumor too."

"O'Shea, sir? He's thick as thieves with the Tammany lot, and I'd like to bet it came from him."

Daniel nodded. "Anyway, there's nothing more we can do about that now, Constable." He stared out into the street. "Do they really think I'd want to stir up the Cosa Nostra again, after my own house was bombed? My family almost killed? It's ludicrous when you come to think about it."

"It sure is, sir. Anyway, it's good to see you sitting up and on the mend. So what did you want to see me about today?"

"It's my wife who needs your help," Daniel said. "Tell him what you need, Molly."

So I explained the story of the children and gave him a description of their missing mother, based on what I thought Emmy would look like when she grew up.

He took down details in a little notebook. "So you want me to check morgue records and possibly the insane asylum for this Margaret Everett Jones, formerly Margaret Montague?"

"That's correct," I said.

"I'll get right onto it," he said. "I'm not on desk duty until tomorrow morning and it all seems pretty quiet at HQ."

Daniel held up a hand. "Listen, Byrne, don't go skipping any normal duty to do this. I don't want you in any trouble because of me."

"Sir, it's an honor to work for you," Byrne said. He saluted, nodded to me, and then turned to go.

❧ Twenty ❧

Thursday, December 21

The next day was one of waiting and hoping. I tried to get into the spirit of Christmas as Bridie helped me set up the tree on the table in the parlor window. We put on the ornaments, starting with the star on top, the candleholders, the fragile glass ones last, then carefully draped the popcorn chain around it. "We must make sure Liam doesn't try to get at this," I said. "It must not look too tempting."

"It looks beautiful." Bridie sighed. "Can't we light the candles now, just to see how they look?"

"Not until Christmas Eve," Daniel's mother said severely.

"But it's three more whole days until Christmas Eve," Bridie said, bending to intercept Liam, who was walking toward the tree with an excited smile on his face.

"I'm glad it is three more whole days," I said. "Because I haven't had time to tell Santa what presents he should bring us."

Bridie grinned. "You don't have to worry. I know all about Santa," she said. "My cousins told me the truth."

They would, I thought. Spoiling a fantasy certainly fit their personality. If I had my way I'd make sure young Malachy got a lump of coal this Christmas. Which reminded me that I'd planned to call on his mother. But that could wait for more pressing things.

"I don't think you should brave the crowds to come shopping with me," I said to Daniel when we were alone in the parlor.

He nodded. "Much as I'd enjoy choosing gifts for my family, I have to admit that I'm not up to it."

"All right. Then maybe I'll go out today and buy Liam and Bridie's gifts," I said. "If you think we can still afford them, that is?" I turned to him with a worried frown. "The police department will pay your hospital bills, won't they? And not cut your pay when you are off work?"

"I hope so," he said. "They certainly have done so in the past. But who knows now? If rumors are circulating that the whole sorry business was my fault, then who knows if I'll even have a job."

"Daniel, this is ridiculous," I exploded. "I've a good mind to go down there and give those men a talking-to they won't forget."

He had to laugh at that. "I'd love to see that, Molly, but it wouldn't do any good." He took my hand. "But in answer to your former question, yes, by all means buy the children their gifts. I've that legacy put by from my father, and I want to make sure their Christmas is a happy one."

So I set off, heading straight for the big FAO Schwarz toy store. This close to the holidays it was a madhouse, with harried-looking attendants scurrying around, being grabbed by impatient customers. Luckily I knew what I wanted. I found the dog on wheels and then selected a small china doll for Bridie. It was really beautiful, with realistic glass eyes and a lacy party dress. *Daniel's mother can teach her to make more clothes*, I thought as I paid and carried my purchases out triumphantly. But that left the more difficult assignment of the day: What to get for Daniel's mother, for Sid and Gus, and for Daniel himself?

I realized I had no hands free to carry anything else and didn't want the doll to get broken, so I took the El back home and managed to sneak the large brown paper parcels up to my bedroom and hide them on top of my wardrobe. Then I went out again, closer to home this time. I decided I couldn't go wrong with books for Sid and Gus, so I went into one of the bookshops around the university and found the perfect thing: a book of recipes from the British Raj. *Delights of India, Ceylon, and Burma*. That should provide them with many happy hours of cooking.

Then I found an illustrated guide to Ireland. I knew that Daniel's mother had been born here right after her parents came from Ireland in the potato famine, but she had never visited the old country. This book had lovely illustrations as well as quaint anecdotes, so I left the store well pleased. Now all that remained was something for Daniel himself. Men are so hard and at the moment I knew it had to be something that would lift his spirits. Spirits—that was a good idea. Daniel did appreciate a good whiskey but rarely treated himself. And I thought of something else. Daniel enjoyed an occasional pipe when he was at repose in his armchair. He had owned a handsome carved wooden tobacco jar before our house burned down. I'd see if I could find a replacement for it. I bought a bottle of whiskey at the liquor store and put off the quest for a tobacco jar for another day.

After lunch Daniel and Liam both went down for their naps, and Daniel's mother helped Bridie finish off the scarf she was knitting for Daniel. I went across the street and found Sid and Gus busy decorating with Tig and Emmy. They too had put up a tree, with exotic ornaments—carved wood tigers from India, glass mirrors, baubles of all sorts. And the table in the center of the parlor had been draped with a white cloth and had a many-branched candlestick on it.

"First night of Hanukkah tonight," Sid said. "Our little guests shall experience a mixture of cultures. This is the menorah I've had since I was a child. I've been over to Hester Street and found a dreidel, and I have my gelt and nuts ready."

"I've never heard of that," I said.

Sid smiled. "Well, I haven't exactly celebrated my Jewish heritage until now, have I? But I used to love it as a child. You spin the top and whichever side it lands on, that is what you win. Gelt is chocolate-covered money. That's the best."

"Bring Bridie and Liam over. They should play it too," Gus said. "And watch Emmy light the first candle. Liam is actually the youngest child, but I wouldn't trust him with a taper yet."

"Absolutely not." I laughed. "He made a beeline for the Christmas tree. We'll have to keep the parlor door shut."

That evening at sundown I took the children over and we all enjoyed the first night of Hanukkah. My mother-in-law was invited, but politely declined. "I see no reason to celebrate a Jewish holiday," she said with strong emphasis on the word "Jewish." I realized that my living in this part of the city had made me far more broad-minded and tolerant than most people, and that for people like my mother-in-law this time of peace and goodwill did not extend to those of a different faith.

We had just sat down to dinner when there was a knock at the door.

"Who now?" Daniel demanded irritably.

I opened the door to find Constable Byrne standing there. "Sorry to disturb you so late, but I was on duty and couldn't get away earlier, Mrs. Sullivan," he said. "But I think I've found the lady you were looking for."

"You have?" I ushered him into the parlor. He commented on the Christmas tree and how festive the room looked while I almost danced with impatience. We had to wait while Daniel made his way slowly down the hall to us, then he handed Daniel a large manila envelope. "This is the description of a young woman pulled from the East River on March 28 this year. It matches the one you gave me completely. And there's even a photograph."

"They take photographs in the morgue these days?" I asked.

"In the case of a suspicious death they do. These days

cameras are everywhere, aren't they? And what a boon. It makes our job so much easier."

"Let me see." Daniel removed a sheet of paper from the envelope. The photograph was not of the best quality, probably taken without a flash, but I could see the resemblance to Emmy immediately—the upturned slant of the eyes and the heart-shaped face. Even in death she looked so peaceful, as if she was asleep, her long blonde hair draped over her shoulders. My immediate reaction was Ophelia, or the Lady of Shalott. There was a sort of timeless, ethereal beauty about her. A lump came into my throat. "Then she did take her own life after all," I said.

"Probably not," Constable Byrne said. "As it turned out, she didn't drown. There was no water in her lungs. She was dead when she was thrown in, so it seems."

"Then why wasn't her death followed up sooner?" I demanded, fighting back the anger that welled up in me.

"Nothing to go on. No identification on her. No laundry marks. Nothing on her clothing. And nobody reported her missing. You can throw someone into the East River wherever you like and eventually the current will bring them down to the docks."

"So her death need not have happened in the city," I said.

"Could have happened anywhere," Daniel agreed. "But you think this is the right woman, do you, Molly?"

"Without a doubt. The likeness to her daughter is striking. And the timing is right. The end of March. That's when she would have disappeared. So she went to find her family and on the way something happened to her."

"And in all likelihood we'll never know what," Constable Byrne said.

I studied the paper. "It doesn't mention any obvious bruising or trauma to her body then?"

The constable clearly winced at a lady calmly discussing such topics.

"I only know what's on this record, Mrs. Sullivan," he said.

I read it through again, carefully, word by word. "It does list the clothing she was wearing," I said. "Light blue cambric dress. Black boots, underclothes . . ." I looked up. "That seems too light to be wearing in March, doesn't it? Where were her outer garments? She'd not have gone out without a coat of some sort."

"I suppose the answer to that is that she died while indoors and was dumped in the river later," Daniel said.

"And nobody reported seeing a body dumped into the river?" I demanded, angry now that Margaret should have come all this way, hopeful for a reunion with her family, only to come to such an ignominious end.

Daniel looked at me with understanding. "There are many places where a body could be dumped without the risk of anyone witnessing. North of here in the marshes— even down on some of the docks."

"From the condition of her face in the photograph she hadn't been in the water long," I said, studying the photograph again. "If she'd been in there for days the fish would have found her."

The young constable turned visibly green.

"I must apologize for my wife, Constable," Daniel said

with a chuckle. "You must realize she was once a detective herself. She has handled some pretty tough cases and now lacks all feminine sensibility to such matters."

"Yes, sir." Constable Byrne nodded. "Will that be all now, sir? Because I need to get home."

"Of course you do. And we can't thank you enough for your kindness," I replied. "At least we know that Margaret Jones came to a tragic end. I just wish it might have been investigated more at the time . . . but with the absence of any identification, I can understand how hard that might be."

I escorted him to the front door. When I returned Daniel was staring at the sheet of paper. "Whoever killed her made sure she wouldn't be identified in a hurry," he said. "Nobody goes out with no identification on them."

"I suppose it could have been in her purse, stolen by robbers who hit her over the head and dumped her in the river," I said. "Something as simple as that."

"It often is," Daniel agreed. "Life is cheap in this city. I've seen people murdered for their boots on a cold day."

I shuddered. In spite of my supposed callousness I still did retain enough feminine sensibilities.

"Do you plan to show this to her children?" Daniel asked.

I stared at the photograph. "I don't think so," I said. "What good would it do? It can't bring their mother back to life. When I've successfully reunited them with their family, then is the time to tell them that their mother is dead. Not before. They've been through enough recently."

Daniel nodded. "You really think that you can reunite them with their family then?"

I sighed. "From all I've been told her father was a harsh and unforgiving sort of person, but even a heart like his should be melted if he once sees his grandchildren. They are so sweet and gentle, Daniel. Who could possibly turn them away?" I waved the photograph at him. "I'll take this to Eustace Everett tomorrow. I was going to see him anyway, to find out what his uncle's reaction was when he was shown Margaret's locket. Now I have more ammunition, and a verification that the photograph really was of her."

"And we only commented a few days ago that for once we'd be able to enjoy a quiet and peaceful Christmas," Daniel said with a tired smile on his face.

I took his hand and held it in my own. "We will, my darling, I promise you," I said.

❊ Twenty-one ❊

Friday, December 22

The next morning I paid an early call on Sid and Gus to tell them what we had learned. The children were sitting at the kitchen table, eating large omelets. They had already lost that fragile and hollow look. Both looked up and beamed when they saw me.

"Do you have any news about Mummy yet?" Tig asked.

"Not yet," I lied. "But I may have news for you really soon."

Then I remembered the fact sheet that Constable Byrne had brought us. "Tell me, Tig. Do you remember what your mother was wearing when she left you?"

"I remember," Emmy piped up. "Her pretty blue dress. It was my favorite."

I smiled. "Blue is my favorite color too," I said. "But eat up your eggs before they get cold. I need to have a word with Miss Goldfarb."

Sid followed me out of the kitchen and into the front parlor. "What is it?" she asked. "You've found out something?"

I nodded, glancing back at the door to make sure nobody could overhear us. "It would appear that their mother's body was pulled from the East River last spring. Anyway the description matches and she was wearing a blue dress. But there was no identification of any kind on her, and the horrible thing is that she didn't drown. She was dead when she was thrown into the water."

"How awful," Sid said. "And the police never found out who did it?"

I shook my head. "Daniel says that given the strength of the current she could have been thrown in anywhere. Nobody of her description was reported missing. So they had nothing to go on."

"Is it possible that the landlady and her friend killed her the way they threatened to do the children?"

"I've been wondering that too. But for what reason, I wonder?"

Sid shrugged. "To rob her of her jewelry, maybe?"

"I don't think she had many worldly goods, Sid. She had eloped with the singing teacher, who was later reduced to working on the docks. I think she only came back here because she was desperate. And anyway," I added, "this body was pulled from the East River. Why would they have taken her across the island when they could have thrown her into the Hudson?"

Sid nodded in agreement at this. "Poor children." She also glanced back toward the door. "Let's just pray that their grandfather relents and takes them in."

"And if he doesn't? What then?" I asked.

"They are so sweet, Molly. No trouble at all. And Gus

has fallen completely in love with them. She said last night it was like a gift from heaven, when she thought she would never have a child of her own."

"It would certainly curtail your lifestyle," I said.

"We'll face that obstacle when we come to it. There are nannies and governesses, you know. And we are not without funds."

All the same, I worried a little as I got ready to visit Eustace Everett on Wall Street. Sid and Gus were so kind and generous, but they were also impulsive and given to whims. Could they really leave the children with a nurse-maid if they decided to go back to Europe or to trek across the Sahara? Still, this might never be a problem after to-day. Mr. Montague would have seen the locket and hope-fully agreed to meet his grandchildren.

"Off again?" my mother-in-law asked, her face a mask of disapproval.

"I've more shopping to do," I lied. "Christmas is only a few days away."

"Anyone would think your husband earned a princely amount the way you are spending," she commented.

"It's Christmas," I replied. "I still need to order the tur-key and we have no candy canes or sugar mice for the tree yet. Just lots of little things, you know. I'm certainly not be-ing extravagant."

I think I heard a *hmmph* sound as I headed for the front door and felt guilty that I had lied to her. It was true I did still have shopping to do, but it would have to wait until more important matters had been taken care of.

The East River looked gray and unfriendly as I walked

down Wall Street toward the Montague Coffee Importers building. The river had actually frozen around the docks and I could hear the sound of ice groaning and grinding with the movement of the water. It sounded as if the river was alive and angry and I shuddered as I thought of Margaret's body floating there. *There will be justice for you,* I thought.

This time I was met immediately by a rather grand young man in a high, stiff collar and black suit. I told him that I'd come to see Mr. Everett.

"I am Phipps, his personal secretary," he said. "May I assist you? Mr. Everett is extremely busy at the moment."

"It is a personal matter and he is expecting me," I said. "Please tell him that Mrs. Sullivan has returned and hopes he has good news for her."

He went away, but returned almost immediately. "Mr. Everett says he is not aware of anyone called Sullivan and has no appointment with you."

"But he saw me only two days ago," I said. "Clearly he has forgotten my name."

I wasn't about to wait any longer, but pushed past him, heading for the stairs. Phipps gave a little cry of surprise and tried to grab my arm. "I'm sorry, madam, but Mr. Everett is extremely busy and has no time to see you today. He has a lot of work to finish before he heads out to Long Island for his engagement party tomorrow."

"I need to speak to him and I'm going to speak to him, and you'll not stop me," I said. Then I pushed past the astonished Phipps, went up the second flight of stairs, and let myself in to Everett's office. The supercilious young man was at his desk again and looked up at me with a frown. "I thought I made it clear to my secretary that I was not to be disturbed," he said. "If this is some kind of charity call, I do not have time today."

"You don't remember me, Mr. Everett? I came to see you two days ago, about your cousin's children. I brought you the locket to give to your uncle."

He stared at me coldly. "Locket? What locket? I've never seen you before in my life."

For a second I was lost for words. "Are you suffering from amnesia?" I demanded angrily. "I brought you a locket that had belonged to your cousin Margaret. You promised to take it to your uncle."

He even managed a smile now. "I'm afraid I have no recollection of any such meeting."

"I'll go and find the young man who escorted me to your office last time," I said. "I have a witness that I was here, don't I?"

"Young man?" He looked puzzled. "The only person you would have met was Phipps. He mans the outer office and ascertains that only legitimate callers are shown up to me. And you've never seen this woman before, have you, Phipps?"

"Never, sir," Phipps answered smoothly.

"It wasn't Phipps. A young man with red hair. Skinny."

"I'm not aware of any such man working here. Are you, Phipps?"

"No, sir," Phipps answered again. "I've been here every day. The lady could not have passed me."

"You see?" Eustace Everett's expression bordered on

triumphant. "Now I suggest you leave before there is any unpleasantness. I understand that they lock away delusional women in the asylum on Ward's Island, and I would hate to see you wind up there. If you don't leave now I will call the police."

I was about to tell him he was welcome to do that. My husband was a senior officer and he'd end up being the one in trouble for stealing my locket. But I swallowed back the words at the last second. My husband was incapacitated at home, and there was a faction in the New York police department who wanted him ousted. I could no longer rely on the police to be on my side.

I forced myself to keep calm. "You will regret this, Mr. Everett," I said. Then I let Phipps usher me down the stairs. I was furious with myself for handing over the locket—the one piece of proof that the children really were Mr. Montague's grandchildren—to a man who obviously would do anything in his power to prevent new heirs from usurping his place. I knew I had taken an instant dislike to him— I saw him as arrogant and self-satisfied. I should have done some investigation into him first—asked Miss Van Woekem what she thought of him. And now he had the locket.

I stood on the bleak waterfront, looking up when a tugboat gave a mournful *toot* nearby. And an awful suspicion crept into my mind. Had Margaret first come to visit him— to sound him out? To ask for his help in smoothing things over with her father? And had he agreed to help her? Offered to escort her to the estate on Long Island, only to kill her along the way and throw her body into the river? But maybe he couldn't bring himself to kill two children, so he had paid Hettie to look after them. Or maybe Hettie and Jack had somehow found out what he had done, and he was paying them for their silence? It seemed all too possible now. And completely unprovable. I seethed with frustration. Was there anything I could do? I could tell Daniel and he might have a bright idea. But Daniel was recovering from a dangerous injury and should not be upset. I could confront Hettie and get the truth out of her, but Jack Hobbs was a dangerous man. I could go to Miss Van Woekem and warn her about her godchild's fiancé. But again it would all be my word against his. If Julia was really in love with him she would hear nothing against him, and I might risk losing the friendship of the old lady.

Besides, presumably Julia would already be out on Long Island, getting ready for her party. And it struck me that maybe I should risk everything by going out there myself, before Eustace could get there and inform the servants that I wasn't to be admitted. There was to be a big party tonight. Could I pose as a guest? The only problem was that there would certainly be a reception line. Eustace would spot me and I'd find myself hauled away by the police. I had to admit that his threat of sending me off to Ward's Island asylum certainly made me think twice about doing anything too risky. I had been to that place to rescue a girl who had been wrongly committed, and I knew how difficult it was to get out again, once one was locked up.

But if I went to the house now, before Eustace arrived . . . might I just have a chance? I had never been out any farther than Brooklyn and Coney Island, and I wasn't even sure if trains went in that direction. Probably not from

Grand Central Terminus, as I didn't think there was a railway bridge across the East River to Long Island. If I crossed the Brooklyn Bridge, would I find a train or a trolley that would take me to the right railroad station? I was horribly conscious of time. Daniel knew some of what I planned to do. I had mentioned Eustace Everett to him. My mother-in-law thought I was out spending Daniel's money. So I would be fine for a while, but I had no idea how long it might take to reach Great Neck. And if I made it that far, what then? All I knew was that it was the Montague estate in Great Neck. Would that be enough to find the place?

I walked back to the nearest El station and asked hopefully at the ticket booth. The ticket agent shook his head with disinterest. "Never had no call to go out to Long Island," he said. "Coney Island. I can tell you how to get there. That's the place to go, in good weather, that is."

"But I need to go to Great Neck," I said.

"Where the swanks live?" He looked at what I was wearing with something like a smirk on his face.

"Never mind." I turned away, biting back frustration.

"Excuse me, ma'am." A man in a business suit tipped his hat to me. "But did I overhear you wanting to take the train out to Great Neck?"

"That's right. Is there any easy way of getting there?"

"Not too bad, if the ice hasn't frozen the points on the train tracks. You get off the El at the Thirty-fourth Street station and there's a ferry across to Hunters Point. The train depot is right there in Long Island City. Make sure you take the Port Washington branch. The train stops in Great Neck."

"Is it very far?"

"Shouldn't take you more than an hour."

"Oh, that's wonderful. Thank you." I beamed at him.

He tipped his hat again and went on his way. I boarded the El, found the ferry across the East River, and was soon standing on the platform waiting for the Port Washington train. Houses soon turned to rural market gardens as we moved away from the city. And then just a bleak expanse of snow with the occasional lonely house or small village clustered around the train station. I began to regret my impulsive behavior. What if I couldn't get back until this evening? What if Eustace arrived and had me arrested? But he had lots of work to do, so he said, so I had at least an hour or two's start on him. I still wasn't sure what I'd say when I showed up at the front door. But then a brilliant idea struck me. There was going to be a big party. They would surely be taking on extra help. I'd go to the back door and try my luck. All I needed was a chance to see Mr. Montague and tell him the truth. That shouldn't take too long. And by the end of the day I might be returning to Tig and Emmy with good news. That bucked me up no end.

❧ Twenty-two ❧

My spirits fell again when I alighted from the train at Great Neck station. Having been told that this was the place where rich people lived I had expected a lively little town, an outpost of civilization. Instead I stood looking at a few dreary houses and goods sheds with no sign of life.

"The Montague estate? Fairview?" the ticket collector asked. "It's about two miles out of town."

"I don't suppose any buses go there, do they?" I asked.

This made him laugh. "It ain't the city, ma'am. What point would there be in a bus? It's only people like the Montagues and their pals who go out there and they all have automobiles to drive themselves. You should see the big, swank automobiles. My, and they drive them so fast. Killed a little kid in Douglaston last year, one of those young gentlemen did. Wrote a check, there and then. As if money could make up for a lost child."

I nodded agreement. "So I've no way of getting out to the estate? No hack I could hire?"

"You may be in luck," he said. "Joe Clancey is supposed to be delivering supplies for their party. I don't think he's left yet. If you go down to your right, you'll see his store."

I was in luck. I found him loading crates of milk into the back of an already full wagon. He was a typical Irishman with a big red face, bright red hair, and side-whiskers. Of course he'd be delighted to give a fellow Irishwoman a ride, he said. I could tell him all about the old country. So the trip passed pleasantly. The narrow road had been cleared of the worst snow and we moved along at a good pace. I made careful note of the route, thinking that I'd have to walk all the way back to the station. Through the skeletons of trees I spotted one impressive house, and then another. But we kept on going. At last we came to a pair of wrought iron gates. They were open and through we went—up to a house that resembled the Palace of Versailles, which I had actually visited that summer. It was hardly less grand, with a fountain playing in spite of the cold and presumably formal gardens now buried under snow. Mr. Clancey drove his wagon around to the back of the house and immediately servants came streaming out to unload it.

"And who might this be?" the cook asked, noticing me as I climbed down from the wagon.

"I'm one of the extra help they requested for the party," I said. "Molly's my name."

"You should have been here two hours ago," she said.

"There was some mix-up," I said. "Another girl couldn't make it and I was only told this morning to get myself out here as soon as possible."

"Well, I expect you're still needed. There's plenty to be done," she said. "Go and find yourself a uniform in the housekeeper's closet and report to her."

Inside was the sort of hustle and bustle that was just short of chaos. Big pots bubbling away in the kitchen. A poor young kitchen maid standing with tears streaming down her cheeks as she chopped a pile of onions. Maids and footmen swept past, carrying wheels of cheese, hams, boxes of petit fours, presumably all ordered from the city. If things progressed at this pace all day I wouldn't have a chance to speak to anyone!

I found a maid's uniform and was just tying my cap when the housekeeper herself appeared. "And you've also been sent from the agency?" she demanded in a voice that wasn't exactly welcoming.

"Yes ma'am," I said. "They came to find me at the last minute. A girl was taken sick, they said." I gave her my best smile. "You must be the housekeeper."

"That's right. I am Mrs. Carter. And your name?"

"Molly, ma'am."

She examined me critically. "You've a nice manner to you. You've worked in a big house before?"

"Oh, yes, ma'am. Several big houses in the city. But I only help out occasionally now that I've a husband and son to take care of. With Christmas coming this seemed too good to turn down."

She actually smiled. "Then you'll know how to clean silver," she said. "Edith is already working on it in the butler's pantry."

"Very good, Mrs. Carter," I said, and almost bobbed a

curtsey before I decided that was taking things too far. I went along a dark hallway and found a skinny young woman working away at a pair of candlesticks.

"Hello," I said. "I'm Molly. They sent me to help you." I looked around at the silver dishes, candelabras, saltcellars, and condiment dishes piled on the table. "You look as if you could do with some help," I added.

" I could indeed," she said. "They stuck me back here, away from all the fun. Here, grab a cloth and there's the tin of polish."

"You're called Edith, are you?" I asked as I started working away at a large dish.

"That's right."

"You been here long, Edith?"

"About a year now. I took over when Fanny left to get married."

"And how is it? Good place to work?"

"It's all right. It's a job."

"It must be hard learning the ropes as the new girl," I went on.

"New girl?" She laughed. "I'm one of the old hands now. Almost all the servants here are new. Mr. Eustace fired everybody and brought in new people when he took over."

"Took over?" I asked. "Is Mr. Montague dead then?"

"No, he lingers on, but they're saying he can't last much longer. And he hasn't been in any state to run things for a while."

I lowered my voice. "It's not for me to say but it seems odd to have a big party when the master lies dying, doesn't it?"

"Does to me too," she whispered back. "But Mr. Eustace was determined to celebrate his engagement and to show his new bride how things are done at Fairview. No expense spared, I can tell you that."

"Is Mr. Montague still in the house? Won't the noise of a party upset him?" I asked.

"They moved him up to the third floor. He has a full-time nurse now and she looks after him. A regular hatchet face, that one. Barks orders as if she was a sergeant major and never a thank you if you do something for her."

"What's Mrs. Carter like?" I asked, still keeping my voice low.

"Not as nice as Mrs. Braithwaite was. She was lovely. It's my belief that the master wouldn't be lying here taking his last breath if she was still around. She cared about him, she really did."

"What happened to her?" I asked.

Edith glanced at the half-open door before replying. "Mr. Eustace gave her the boot last spring. He said she was disrespectful to him and had been snooping. So she was out, after being here for thirty years. I know the master wouldn't have liked it if he'd been well enough to know what was going on."

"Where is she now?" I asked.

"She lives with her son in Great Neck. He's opened an automobile repair shop there, on account of how many people around here drive automobiles. Can you imagine that a man could make a living fixing automobile engines? Whatever next."

I put my dish, now sparkling, to join the others and

started on some saltcellars. Having been assigned to this task, I could hardly leave Edith to it. So I worked as quickly as I could. At least I'd already learned some interesting facts, but my journey would be wasted if I couldn't see Mr. Montague in person. From what Edith said, it sounded as if he might no longer be compos mentis.

At last we finished the silver and I went back into the kitchen to find other servants eating their midday meal. There was a big tureen of vegetable soup as well as slices of ham, cold roast beef, bread, and pickles on the table.

"It's catch as catch can today," the cook said. "I've no time to make our food, so grab, eat, and get back to work."

I helped myself and was nearly finished when the cook said, "Ruby, put that down and take up the master's hot milk."

I jumped up before she could react. "She's only just sat down," I said. "I'd be happy to take it up for her. I've finished."

"That's nice of you, young lady. Very charitable. I don't know if they told you but they moved the master out of his normal suite up to the third floor so that the noise doesn't bother him too much tonight."

"I'll find my way, thank you." I picked up the cup and found the back stairs that servants always use. My feet echoed in the narrow stairwell as I went up and up. I was quite out of breath by the time I came to the third floor and opened the door onto a rather Spartan hallway. It was completely silent and I tiptoed forward, not knowing which door to open. I had discovered two unused bedrooms and a small kitchen with a spirit stove before I tried the door at the end of the hall and found myself in Mr. Montague's bedroom. There he was, lying on a narrow bed, looking so pale and unmoving that at first I thought he was dead. Then I saw his sheet rise and fall to gentle breathing. Fast asleep then. There was a fire burning in the grate and the room had the sweet, cloying smell of sickness to it. Did I dare to wake him—to tell him my real mission and show him the picture I hoped was of his daughter?

I stood there with the cup of hot milk in my hand, unable to make up my mind. If I woke him and showed him the picture, it might give him such a shock that it killed him. But the news of grandchildren might give him hope to keep on living and get well again.

"What do you think you are doing, girl?" a sharp voice demanded. A tall, thin woman in a severe dark blue uniform stood there, glaring at me.

I spun around, almost slopping milk into the saucer. "I'm sorry," I whispered, "I was told to bring up Mr. Montague's hot milk. I didn't know where to go."

"Never disturb Mr. Montague. Now you know, don't you?" she snapped. "I've told them in the kitchen before— the milk gets put in that anteroom next door. I've a little stove there to warm it up again when Mr. Montague awakes."

"I'll put it there now," I said. I glanced back at him. "Poor Mr. Montague," I said. "This must be so distressing for everyone."

"We all have to die sometime," she said. "And what did he have to live for?"

There was no hint of compassion in her face, and I wondered who had chosen such an unfeeling creature as Mr. Montague's nurse when presumably he could afford the best care. Eustace Everett, of course, I decided. He'd be only too happy if his uncle died and he inherited the estate, the business, the wealth. Then I took this thought one step further: If he had really killed his cousin, could he now be actively working to kill his uncle? I followed the hostile nurse to the little kitchen and put the cup on the counter. An empty cup and saucer stood there, along with several medicine bottles.

"Would you like me to take this cup down to be washed?" I asked.

"No. Leave it," she snapped. "Go back where you're needed." Then she spun around as a moan came from Mr. Montague's room. "Coming, sir," she called. "Just fetching your milk.

"Go on. Off with you." She stood there, glaring at me, waiting for me to leave. I headed to the stairwell, but as soon as her back was turned I doubled back, creeping close to the wall. I was just in time to watch her take the lid off a tin and carefully spoon something into the milk, then stir it up. And I just had time to flatten myself in a dark doorway as she came through with the cup to Mr. Montague's room.

Now my suspicions were completely roused. Of course the powder that she had stirred into his drink could be nothing more than sugar, glucose, or some kind of fortifying mixture. But the way she had snapped at me when I offered to take away the empty cup was ringing alarm bells. I knew I had to act quickly. I tiptoed into the anteroom and took out my handkerchief. I carefully spooned some of the contents of the tin into the handkerchief, wrapped it carefully, and tucked it into my pocket. Then I hurried to the back staircase before the nurse could see me.

It seemed like a good time to make my escape. I realized I'd have no chance to talk to Mr. Montague in his current state, and I'd learned all I was likely to learn with a house full of new servants. Besides, I wanted to visit his old housekeeper, Mrs. Braithwaite, before I took the train back to the city.

I came down the stairs and out into the servant's hallway. A quick visit to the uniform closet and I was in my own clothes again. Making my exit through the back door wasn't quite so easy. The door was beside the kitchen, where any number of people were working. That left me only one choice—to try my luck through the front. I retrieved a candlestick, pushed open the baize door, and was "above stairs." The floors were marble, dotted with fine Persian rugs. There were classical statues in niches and large potted palms. I passed a footman who looked at me with surprise.

"I was told this candlestick was needed in the dining room," I said, holding it out to him.

"I don't know who told you that," he said, taking it from me. "These candlesticks are for the morning room where they'll be putting the presents. Honestly it's chaos. Nobody seems to know what they are doing today. I'll be surprised if the party isn't a complete disaster." And he flaunted off, brandishing the candlestick, leaving me alone in the main hall. I had just reached the front door unnoticed and unhindered when I heard the crunch of wheels and muffled thud of hoofbeats on the snowy drive and a fine carriage came to a halt. I was trapped, standing on the front steps, not able to run and not wanting to retreat back inside. My worst fear was that Eustace himself had arrived, but when the coachman sprang down to open the door, he helped out a pretty and very young woman.

"Hello," she said when she saw me. "Don't tell me you're one of my guests? You're really, really early."

I toyed with telling her I was a friend of her godmother, but realized I wasn't exactly dressed to impress. "Oh, no, miss," I said. "I was sent to deliver a present from the city."

"A present? How exciting." She beamed at me. "What is it? Do tell."

"I'm not allowed to say, miss," I replied coyly. "And it should be opened with your fiancé, shouldn't it?"

"I suppose so. Isn't it fun getting engaged and married?"

Then she skipped up the front steps like a small child. I turned away feeling overwhelming pity. How could a bright and lively young thing like her find herself tied to such an objectionable man as Eustace Everett? And an even darker thought crept into my mind. If he was marrying her for her fortune, would she also end up having a mysterious accident or illness?

⚙ Twenty-three ⚙

A s I started back to the railway station I rather wished I had told her I was a friend of her god-mother's. Then she might have offered me the use of her carriage to take me to the station. Instead I was in for a long walk in the bitter cold. And snow was starting to fall gently too. But I was in luck again. As I passed the gates of another mansion, a butcher's delivery wagon was coming out. I flagged him down and was back in the hamlet of Great Neck in no time at all. It was easy enough to find Bert's Automobile Repairs and from there to be directed to his house, where I hoped to find his mother, Mrs. Braith-waite. She answered the door herself, a pleasant-looking older woman, wearing a floury apron.

"Sorry, but you've caught me in the midst of Christmas baking," she said.

"I won't take up much of your time but I need your help," I said. "It's about Margaret Montague."

"Margaret?" Her face lit up. "You've news of her? I've been so worried."

"I think I do have news, but it may not be all good," I

said. "My name is Mrs. Sullivan. And I've just come from Fairview."

She brushed down her hands on her apron. "Come in, do. In the kitchen, if you don't mind. I've a pecan pie I can't let burn."

The small kitchen was delightfully warm and she poured me a welcome cup of coffee.

"You've heard from Margaret, have you?" she asked.

"I'm currently looking after her children," I said, and started to tell her the whole story.

"Out begging on the streets? Poor little mites," she interrupted. "That doesn't sound like Margaret at all. She'd never have abandoned her children. She was always such a kind and warm girl. You just had to love her. I was so fond of her myself. It broke my heart when the master said we were never to mention her name again."

"Tell me, Mrs. Braithwaite," I said. "Do you think Mr. Montague would still react the same way if he met his grandchildren?"

"I don't believe he would, ma'am," she said. "In fact in later years, he said to me once, 'Maybe I was too hasty, Maude. Now I have no one.'" She looked at me with sadness in her eyes. "And now I understand he might be dying. Poor man."

"Was he sick when you left Fairview?"

"He wasn't well, but nothing like I've heard recently. They say he has a full-time nurse."

I didn't share my suspicions about the nurse but instead I said, "The nurse wasn't there when you were dismissed then? Exactly when was that?"

"This spring. March, it was. I couldn't believe it when Mr. Eustace told me. He claimed I'd been disrespectful and he wanted someone with more modern ideas than me. But I think it was on account of the letter."

"Letter?" I asked.

She nodded. "A letter came for Mr. Montague. I saw it on the salver in the front hall, and I thought I recognized Miss Margaret's handwriting. I was going to take it straight up to the master but Mr. Eustace arrived. 'I think this might be from Miss Margaret,' I said. And he said, 'You know we've been forbidden to mention her name again. Give that to me. It would only upset my uncle.' And he took it and stuffed it into his pocket. And right after that I was told my services were no longer needed."

"How sad," I said. "Margaret wrote to her father. She might have been welcomed back and still been alive now."

"You're sure she's dead?" Mrs. Braithwaite asked.

I opened my handbag and took out the photograph. When she saw it she put her hand to her mouth and gave a little cry. "Oh, my poor darling girl," she said. "Do they know what happened to her? What fiend did this?"

"She was fished from the East River, but she was already dead when someone threw her body in," I said. "And between the two of us, Mrs. Braithwaite, I can't help wondering if Eustace Everett didn't engineer the whole thing. If he'd retrieved the letter he could have written to Margaret in New York, telling her to meet him, that he'd drive her out to see her father. And on the way he killed her."

She looked at me with horror. "Surely not, ma'am? I mean I've never really taken to Mr. Eustace, even before

I was dismissed without a thank you. But a murderer? He's family, after all."

"Family with a lot to lose," I said. "Tell me, do you remember a locket that Margaret wore?"

"Of course." Her face lit up again. "A pretty little thing with pearls around the outside and her initials on it. Her mother had it made for her christening with a lock of Margaret and David's baby hair inside. After her mother died she never took it off."

"We had that locket until a couple of days ago," I said, and related the whole interaction with Eustace.

She gasped with shock. "Then the man is evil incarnate. Make sure you watch over those precious children well, Mrs. Sullivan. Who knows what he'll do next?"

Until then it hadn't actually occurred to me that the children might be in danger. I felt a great urgency to rush home and make sure they were safe. "I should be going," I said. "I've taken enough of your time, and I need to get back to my own family in the city."

"You won't stay and have a bite of pie?" she said. "It will be out of the oven in a minute or two."

"As tempting as that is, I really should go," I said. "I'm so glad we've had this talk. It confirmed everything I have suspected." As I got up I thought of something else. "Margaret's brother, David. I understand he died in a riding accident?"

"He did, very tragic. He was a reckless boy, fun-loving, but with such a good heart. There was no malice to him."

"It was definitely an accident, was it?"

"Oh, yes. He fell when his horse was jumping a gate."

Then her expression changed. "There was something strange, now that you mention it," she said. "One of the grooms. Simpson, his name was. He claimed that he thought the girth had been tampered with—almost cut through. But he liked his tipple and he was dismissed for negligence right away. But after what you've told me, he might have been right."

"But Mr. Eustace wasn't there at the time, surely?"

"Oh, yes he was, ma'am. He came to live at Fairview right after Margaret eloped with the singing teacher. He'd been out riding with David."

"I must get back," I said. "I have to do something before it's too late."

"Do you think you can do anything, Mrs. Sullivan?" she asked.

"I'll give it a darned good try," I replied. "And Mrs. Braithwaite—don't tell anyone that you had this little talk with me. I wouldn't want you put into any kind of danger."

The train ride back to the Long Island terminus seemed to drag on forever. I was impatient to make sure the children were safe, and to bring Eustace Everett to justice. In my mind I saw how he orchestrated the whole thing since coming to his uncle's house. First by planning the death of David, the heir, then by firing all the old retainers and bringing in new servants. And finally by putting Mr. Montague's care in the hands of a nurse whom I suspected of gradually killing him. I realized that none of this could be proven unless the sample of medicine I had concealed in my handkerchief was indeed some kind of drug or poison.

I was never more relieved to be walking up Patchin Place. The family was assembled in the kitchen, eating some of the fruits of my mother-in-law's latest baking. The aromas of cinnamon and spice and freshly baked bread were intoxicating. Daniel was sitting at the table with a pillow in his back. "Well, there you all are," I said, beaming at them as I took off my scarf and gloves.

"I hope you told them we wanted a big plump one," Daniel's mother said, looking up from the stove.

I had no idea what she was saying, until she added. "The turkey. You went out to order the turkey from the butcher, if I remember rightly. And to do some shopping, but I don't see any packages."

"I might not want you to see any packages," I said, smiling mysteriously. "I might have left them across the street."

"Those street children have been over here for most of the day," Daniel said. "They've played very nicely, I must say. Good kids."

"But they are safely back with Sid and Gus now, are they?" I asked, terrified that something might have happened to them. It was only as I said it that I realized I might have given myself away, having claimed to have dropped off packages there. But nobody seemed to notice anything amiss.

"Only left maybe fifteen minutes ago," Daniel's mother said. "Miss Walcott came to fetch them."

I let out a sigh of relief. They were safe. And I reminded myself that Eustace Everett would be on his way out to Long Island for his engagement party. He'd have no time to kidnap his little cousins.

"And Daniel had a visitor today, didn't you, boy?" his mother said. "Such a strange-looking man. Almost comical."

I turned to Daniel. "Someone connected with a case I've been working on," he said, but I saw in his eyes that I should leave the subject alone. "Perhaps you'd help me back to the front parlor," he said. "I think I've been sitting up long enough."

I took his arm and walked him back down the hall, made him comfortable on the sofa, then put more coal on the fire. He waited until I'd done this before he said in a low voice, "You'll never guess who came to visit me today. Monk Eastman, no less."

"Monk Eastman?" I couldn't have been more surprised. "What did he want?"

"A favor, actually," he said. "He's out on bail on a robbery charge. Small potatoes compared to most of the things he's done. But they've been able to pin this one on him. He won't get off."

"So he'll go to jail?"

"I fear so. But he wanted me to put in a good word for him and make sure it's not for too long."

"Will you do that? He's a ruthless gang leader, after all."

"But I can deal with him, Molly. We understand each other. Not like these Italians." He looked at me and grinned. "Monk was horrified I'd been shot and asked me if I'd like his boys to teach those Italians who shot me a lesson they wouldn't forget in a hurry. I told him no fighting between gangs, if he wants me to smooth things over for him."

"Quite right," I said.

"And I also told him I'd heard he was using Junior Eastmans as pickpockets. That had to stop right away. He claimed to know nothing about it, of course, but he said if he heard any of his boys were pickpocketing there would be all hell to pay."

"So I don't have to go and see Nuala to make sure Malachy behaves himself," I said, relieved that there was one chore less in my future. I sat on the sofa beside Daniel. "But I do have something I want you to do for me, Daniel." And I told him exactly what I'd been doing all day.

He looked shocked, annoyed. "This isn't your business, Molly," he said.

"Of course it is. Those children are being kept from their grandfather by a man who probably killed their mother."

"You can't prove that."

"I know. But I can prove that he took the locket and then denied ever meeting me before. And he's hired a nurse who puts something into his uncle's milk. I've brought a sample home in my handkerchief. You have chemists working for the police who could analyze this, don't you?"

He frowned. "Yes, but it could take some time, and it is the weekend before Christmas tomorrow. I don't know whether folks will be working as usual. And the case isn't even in our jurisdiction. It would be for the county sheriffs out on Long Island to investigate."

I had had a long and strenuous day. I had taken risks, walked through the snow, and I had reached the limits of my patience. "Dammit, Daniel," I snapped. "It's a man's life that's at stake here. If you'll not help me, I'll do it on my own. The Northern Dispensary on Christopher Street will have a druggist working there. Maybe he'll know how to analyze it for me, or can suggest someone who can do it. I'll go right now."

"Molly, calm down." Daniel grabbed my wrist with surprising strength. "All right. I'll try to think of someone. We usually use a Dr. Harrington at the university, but they will be away for their winter recess, won't they? I suppose a porter or someone will be on duty and might know where Dr. Harrington lives. Apart from that I'm not sure. I can't send the sample to headquarters to go through the usual channels because it's not my case. It's not even the NYPD's case. It would only get me into more hot water . . ." He paused and gave an apologetic shrug.

"Write me a note to give Dr. Harrington," I said testily. "I'll go out immediately and try to track him down before he escapes for the holiday."

I brought him ink and notepaper and then set off for the university. I did find a porter who informed me he was sure he'd overheard Dr. Harrington saying that he was going to his family in Massachusetts for a well-earned rest. I bit back my frustration as I walked away. *Would there be somebody at the Northern Dispensary who might have the skills?* I wondered. But they were always so busy as they were the main outpatient facility for this whole area of the city. Then it hit me—I did know a compounding chemist. I had once helped in a case involving a Vassar friend of Sid and Gus who worked for a pharmacist. Mr. McPherson was not the most pleasant of men but probably competent enough. Unfortunately his pharmacy was on the Upper West Side. I had already traveled more than I wanted to today. But a man's life was at stake. I sighed as I made for the El station and took the train uptown.

The Upper West Side was in full festive mood as I came down from the El onto Broadway. A brass band was playing "God Rest Ye Merry Gentlemen." Hawkers were selling toys and knickknacks. Young girls carried trays of holly and mistletoe sprigs and the butcher's window was full of plump chickens, turkeys, and geese. The scent of roasting chestnuts made my mouth water. As I approached the pharmacy I saw to my dismay that the blinds were in the process of being pulled down. The door was locked. I rattled the handle and knocked loudly. After a moment the door was unlocked and Mr. McPherson himself glared at me.

"We're already closed," he said. Then he studied my face. "I know you," he said.

"You do," I said. "It was Miss Murphy then. Now it's Mrs. Sullivan. I helped Emily when she was involved in that unpleasant business with your assistant."

"So you did." His harsh expression softened a little. "But she's not here today. She's spending Christmas with her father. Getting along like a house on fire, those two."

"I'm so glad," I said. "And so pleased she's still working for you."

"Turning out to have a fine head on her shoulders," he said grudgingly. "Will make a good pharmacist one day."

So he was finally letting her train in his profession. At any other time I'd have been pleased to chat, but the pressure of time was overwhelming. "Please give her my best when you see her," I said. "And I'm so sorry to intrude like this just before Christmas. But it's really another matter of life or death and I didn't know who I could turn to." I took a deep breath while he glared at me suspiciously.

"I have reason to believe that a man is being poisoned and I wondered if you have the means to analyze what is in a medication that is being administered to him."

His eyebrows shot up in surprise. "Being poisoned, you say?"

"Or at least being drugged," I said, and related how his nurse had added some of the powder to his hot milk and not allowed me to touch the empty cup.

"I managed to take away a sample," I said, and produced my handkerchief.

"I'll do what I can." He took it gingerly. "I can't promise anything, mind you, but I do know that you're not some hysterical female prone to fancies. If you think foul play is involved, then it might well be."

I handed him my card and begged him to send a message to my husband as soon as he discovered anything. On my way to the El station I stopped to buy two small wooden toys for Tig and Emmy—a puppet on a stick and pecking ducks. Then I faced the long ride back home, aboard a train that had once almost killed me. I felt completely exhausted by the time I came down to Greenwich Avenue and just remembered at the last minute that I hadn't yet ordered the turkey. I was in luck and the butcher still had some fine plump ones. I paid for a fourteen-pounder and asked that it be delivered to us the next day. My feet would hardly obey me as I trudged up Patchin Place.

"My goodness, girl, you look all in," Daniel's mother said

as I came into the kitchen. "But never mind. There's a fish pie in the oven, seeing that it's Friday, and the tea is still hot."

"I'm sorry I've left you with so much to do," I said, and decided to come clean with her—well, almost clean. "As well as the Christmas shopping I've been trying to reunite those children with their family and it hasn't been easy."

"Family? Here?" She looked up sharply. "I thought they came from England. At least judging by their accents."

"Their mother was from here originally."

"And you've located their kinfolk?"

"I have, but they might not be welcome, so I'm having to tread carefully."

She shook her head. "Molly Murphy Sullivan, you take on too much. You've a family of your own. You don't need the cares of the world on your shoulders or you'll run yourself into an early grave."

"But those poor little orphans," I said. "You've seen them yourself. If you had a chance to help them, wouldn't you do it?"

She sighed. "I suppose so. Now go and see if your man wants to join us for supper."

⚓ Twenty-four ⚓

Saturday, December 23

The next day I waited impatiently for news from my chemist. My first task was to seek out a new tobacco jar for Daniel's Christmas present. I found a splendid one in polished cherry wood. Then, pleased with myself, I went to the market for vegetables for the holiday, since tomorrow was Sunday and everything would be closed. Then I stopped at the candy shop for Christmas treats. When I came home, my conscience was nagging me that it was about time I did some Christmas baking. Apart from the Christmas pudding, Daniel's mother had done it all so far. I tried to think what we still needed that might be within the realm of my cooking skills. "What do we still need for Christmas?" I asked. "Gingerbread? Cookies?"

"I think we already have enough food to feed an army," Daniel's mother commented. "I've the last of the mince pies in the oven now."

"I feel badly that you have done all the work," I said.

"Not at all. It's good to be able to cook for the family again. And at my house Martha always does the cooking. I've enjoyed myself."

"And I'm extremely grateful," I said. "Your baking is so much better than mine."

"You'll get better as you go along and you've a bigger family to feed," she said. "I wasn't so hot myself in the first years of marriage."

I paced the house, waiting for word from the chemist, wanting to be useful, picking up toys, dusting surfaces that didn't need dusting. I felt frustration boiling over. If no poisonous substance could be found in that powder then I'd be powerless. The old man would die and Eustace would inherit the estate. And the children would never meet their grandfather.

In the afternoon Tig and Emmy came over to our house again, as Sid and Gus were preparing the house to entertain friends. The children had a merry time together. Watching Emmy dancing around and singing with Bridie, it was hard to picture her as the pathetic little waif huddled in the doorway. Her cheeks were now rosy and there was a sparkle in her eyes.

As I watched her I was trying to think how I could possibly catch out Eustace Everett. I was convinced he had killed his cousin Margaret, but I couldn't come up with any way I'd be able to prove it, given that she could have been thrown into the river anywhere along its length and carried by the current for miles. If only my chemist Mr. McPherson could find some kind of poison or drug . . .

At last I could stand it no longer. There was something

I could do. I would go and talk to Hettie Jenkins. I put on my overcoat and scarf.

"You're going out again?" Mrs. Sullivan asked.

"I've thought of a couple of little things," I said. "I won't be long."

The streets were packed with shoppers carrying baskets laden with provisions, stacks of packages. Everyone was doing last-minute Christmas preparation and there was a feeling of excitement and gaiety in the air. Children were standing on street corners singing carols for pennies. Delivery boys forced their way through the crowd carrying great turkeys and geese and hams. It was hard not to be caught up in the festive mood, and as I neared Mrs. Jenkins's boardinghouse, I asked myself whether this was a wise move. I had promised Daniel I wouldn't do anything dangerous. If Jack Hobbs was there, I'd find an excuse to leave.

The house looked more rundown and forbidding in the gloomy light. Heavy clouds threatened more snow and the wind off the Hudson cut like a knife. I almost turned around and went away again. But those children deserved the truth. I banged on the front door but there was no reply. I'm afraid I heaved a sigh of relief that it had not been opened by Jack Hobbs. Then it occurred to me that Mrs. Jenkins would be doing what the rest of the world was today—her last-minute shopping for the holidays.

I walked away, standing at a distance to see if a curtain twitched and I was being observed, but nothing moved. Then I started prowling the shops on the surrounding streets. At last I was in luck. I watched her coming out of the butcher's with a basket covered in a cloth. I decided that a crowded street was the very best place to confront her. I went up to her.

"Why, Mrs. Jenkins," I said. "Just the person I was looking for."

She stared at me, frowning. "Who are you?"

"Don't you remember? I came to your place to take a look at a room?"

"Ah, yes. Will you be wanting it now?"

"I think not. And I was also the first person to take an interest in the children."

"And what children would they be?" she asked.

"The ones that Eustace Everett paid you to look after."

I did get a reaction to that. She almost stumbled on a clump of snow, then picked up her pace, pushing through the crowd. I hurried to keep up with her.

"So I'm curious," I said. "Did he want them kept alive because he was too softhearted to kill two innocent children?"

She shot me a swift glance. "Him? Softhearted?" And she made a sound that was halfway between a snort and a laugh. Then she realized, of course, what she had said.

"Thank you," I replied. "You've made this very easy for me. I'll be passing along the information to my husband, the police captain."

"You've got nothing on me," she said defiantly. "I took those children in and fed them out of the goodness of my heart. There's no crime in that."

"No, you're not to blame if someone paid you to look

after two children, even if you did take his money and then send the children out into the streets to beg. But, as you say, it's not a crime."

"Then leave me alone and stop bothering me," she said, shouldering her way past two women, who turned to glare at her.

I stepped out into the street, getting my feet wet in the muddy gutter, and drew level with her again. We were now approaching her house. Any minute now she'd go inside and slam the door on me. Jack Hobbs might even be there now.

"As I said, it's no crime. However, being implicated in the murder of their mother—now that's another matter."

She spun around and for a moment there was a look of terror in her eyes. "What are you saying? That I killed their mother? I had nothing to do with that. Nothing, do you hear?"

"Mr. Everett might say that you did, to save his own skin. How else did you get your hands on the locket she never took off? I wouldn't be surprised if the police didn't come to the conclusion that she was killed in your house and then dumped in the river."

"No." She was shaking her head violently now. "No. That's a lie. It wasn't like that at all." She looked up and I heard a sigh of relief escape from her. "Jack!" she called. "Thank God you're back. This woman is making all kinds of accusations. Tell her I never . . ."

But I had decided that discretion was the better part of valor. I dodged back into the crowd, slipped into the crowded grocer's shop, and watched as they looked for me, then went off home. At least I'd given them something to think about. At least I knew the truth, that Eustace Everett had been paying her to keep the children. Until when? Until his uncle died and he took over the estate and the business? But if it was found that he had been trying to poison his uncle, I could now have Hettie Jenkins called in as a witness, and in spite of her hard outer shell, I suspected she'd crack quite easily to save her own skin.

I bought some mistletoe from a boy on the street then came home to find everyone at the tea table. Tig and Emmy went back across the street. We ate supper and put the children to bed.

Around eight o'clock there was a tap on the door. I leaped up, convinced it would be news from the pharmacy. But instead it was Gus. "Molly, dearest," she said. "We have a few friends over and it's all very jolly and we wondered if you would like to join us. Daniel too if he feels up to it, of course."

I glanced into the parlor where Daniel and his mother were sitting. "I don't think I should desert my dear ones, however tempting it sounds," I said with a smile. "But thank you for the invitation."

"If you change your mind, you know where to find us," she said. "Ryan is there and asking after you."

Ryan O'Hare, flamboyant Irish playwright, was one of my favorite people.

"I'll test the waters," I said, and closed the front door.

"Was that Miss Walcott?" asked my ever sharp mother-in-law. "Everything all right?"

"They are having a small gathering of friends and wanted

to know if we'd like to join them," I said. "I told them Daniel wasn't up to it yet."

"You should go," Daniel said. "You enjoy their kind of socializing."

I looked from him to his mother. "If you don't mind? I'd just pop in for a little while."

"Daniel and I will keep each other company," his mother said. "We'll do some reminiscing about the good times when his father was alive."

"Fine, then." I smiled, ran upstairs to change into a more respectable gown, and then put on a shawl to cross the street. "I won't stay long."

Gus's face lit up when she answered the front door. "You're here. That's splendid. Come on in," she said. "As you can tell, the party is in full swing."

Her words were almost drowned out by the loud laughter coming from her front parlor. I felt suddenly hesitant, as one does being introduced into a lively company. Now that I was a wife and mother I rarely went to social functions at night. I was definitely out of practice. Faces looked up at me, some of them curious, some smiling in recognition. Ryan leaped to his feet and came toward me. His outfit no longer shocked me—a white shirt with frills, a black-velvet waistcoat and tight black-velvet trousers. He looked like a stage pirate, or Lord Byron, back from the grave. "The love of my life returns to me," he said. "I have been quite wasting away pining for you, my darling Molly."

"I see you're still full of blarney," I said, laughing as he grabbed me around the waist. "Since when have I ever been the love of your life?"

"I'm cut to the quick," he replied. "I just hope that brute is treating you well and not beating you too often," he remarked, leading me to sit beside him on the sofa.

Sid introduced me rapidly to those I didn't know. Gus put a glass of hot-buttered rum into my hand. It was all so jolly and carefree, until I remembered that upstairs in bed were two children whose futures were still uncertain.

"Someone told me that you two had become parents," a male guest commented. "More virgin births at Christmas?"

Amid the laughter Sid explained the circumstances. "But Molly is hoping to reunite them with their family," she added.

"That won't be so easy if Eustace Everett has his way," I said.

"Eustace Everett?" Ryan looked at me, an amused twinkle in his eyes.

"Do you know him?"

"Not my bosom friend exactly," he said, "but let's just say we frequent the same club."

"I'm surprised any New York club would admit you, Ryan," Sid said.

"God forbid, not that kind of club," he said, laughing. "Do you think I would ever be seen dead inside one of those stuffy men's clubs? The club I'm referring to is a more private sort of affair . . . where gentlemen like me go to . . . meet other gentlemen like me. It's called the Stallion Club."

There was more laughter and ribald remarks.

"And you've seen Eustace Everett there?" I asked.

Ryan was still chuckling. "Frequently, darling. Always

hoping to make a lucky connection, but of course he never stands a chance with gorgeous chaps like me around."

I stared into the flames of the fire, trying to suppress my grin. Eustace Everett at a homosexual club! *I have you now,* I thought in triumph.

When I came home a little later I was still trying to decide how to make the best use of this newfound information. I could confront him with it, but that really would be playing with fire. If he had killed Margaret and her brother and was currently poisoning his uncle, I might not live to regret my action. Then I came up with a brainwave: I would go to Miss Van Woekem and tell her everything. She was Julia's godmother. She would not want her to enter into a marriage with a man who would only cause her grief. I resolved to visit her first thing the next morning. I shared my intention with Daniel as we lay in bed together that night. For once he made no objection, but added, "As long as it's just Miss Van Woekem, and you let her make up her mind what to do with this knowledge."

"Of course," I said sweetly.

I had forgotten it was Sunday as well as Christmas Eve. Mrs. Sullivan greeted me with her hat on. "Is the mass still at eight o'clock?" she asked. "You'll need to hurry and get those children ready."

Oh, dear. I couldn't tell her that I only went to mass if she was visiting. "I think I'll leave Liam with his father," I said. "Daniel's certainly not going to go to mass today. But I'll make sure Bridie is ready to go with you."

"With me?" She raised an eyebrow. "You'll not be coming yourself then?"

"Someone should help Daniel dress and feed him breakfast," I said.

"Daniel would not want you to miss your Sunday obligations," she said frostily. "That was not how we raised him."

I gave in. It was easier to go to mass than to create a scene. I got Bridie ready quickly, put on my coat, scarf, hat, and gloves, and we walked down to Washington Square. It was freezing cold in the early morning and the clouds were heavy with the promise of more snow soon. The church was not much warmer—small oil heaters dotted around did little to take off the chill and the congregation huddled together, trying to keep warm. Luckily the priest wanted to be through as quickly as we did and rushed through the mass at breakneck speed, earning another complaint from my mother-in-law as we walked home.

"I've never heard the Holy Mass said with such irreverence," she said. "Like a galloping horse that man was."

I smiled to myself. When we got home I helped Daniel wash and get dressed, washed and dressed my son, then cooked flapjacks and bacon before I made my escape. "I'm going to visit Miss Van Woekem," I announced as I cleared away the breakfast things.

"And the roast for Sunday lunch?" Mrs. Sullivan asked, already with a look of disapproval on her face. "You're planning to be back in time to serve a roast, I've no doubt?"

"It should go into the oven at eleven if I'm not back by then," I said. "I'll peel the potatoes first and have the cabbage ready in the saucepan."

"Anyone would think you cared more for that old lady than your own family," Mrs. Sullivan muttered as I went about my work.

"It's not entirely a social call," I said. "I heard something last night that she should know. Something about her god-daughter's intended."

"Spreading gossip is not wise or healthy." She scooped the cabbage stalks into the waste bucket.

"It's more than gossip, I'm afraid. It's criminal behavior and she needs to be told about it before it's too late."

She stood in front of me, her hands on her hips. "Why you have to concern yourself with other people's lives is something I'll never understand," she said. "Is your son going to grow up getting a brief glimpse of you occasionally? I thought you agreed to give up this ridiculous detective work when you married, but it seems to me you're carrying on with it more than ever."

"I'm really not," I said, fighting to keep a pleasant expression on my face. "All of this has to do with Tig and Emmy. You'd like to see them reunited with their family, wouldn't you? And the man who killed their mother brought to justice?"

"You think you can do that?"

"I hope so," I said.

"Well, you'd better get going then," she said. I kissed my son, my husband, and Bridie, and off I went. Gramercy Park lay sleeping under a snowy blanket. A couple of carriages stood at the curb, their horses and drivers looking sorry for themselves in the bitter cold. I knocked at Miss Van Woekem's door and was admitted by a surprised maid.

"She doesn't normally accept callers at this hour," the maid said, and ushered me into the smaller back parlor, where the old lady sat with a shawl around her shoulders, reading the morning newspaper.

I apologized for my visit, but told her she'd realize why I had to come straight away. Then I related the whole story—everything I knew and everything I suspected. She was a good listener and said not a word, her head on one side like an attentive sparrow, as I talked.

"Some of this I can prove," I said. "Some I can't. Until we know what was in that powder that is being tested I can't go to the police. But I do know that he took the children's locket and then denied it to my face. And I do know that he frequents a club for homosexuals. And that he intercepted a letter to Mr. Montague from his daughter. And dismissed the housekeeper right afterward."

She picked up a little bell on the table and rang it fiercely. I thought I was about to be thrown out, that I had crossed a line by besmirching the name of Julia's intended, but when her maid came in the old lady said, "Help me up, girl. Fetch my coat and hat. And tell Sims to bring round the carriage."

"You're going out, ma'am?" the maid asked.

"That should be quite obvious. Now get a move on, girl. We haven't all day to waste."

"Where are you going, Miss Van Woekem?" I asked.

She looked surprised that I didn't know. "We're going to see that justice is served," she said.

❧ Twenty-five ❧

An ancient but impressive carriage pulled up in front of the house. Miss Van Woekem arranged her fur around her shoulders and was helped inside. I climbed in beside her and tucked the rug over her knees.

"And where do we find these children?" she asked me. "We'll need to take them with us. Mr. Everett will not have the nerve to turn me away."

So we went first to Patchin Place. Tig and Emmy were bundled up and wrapped in rugs, then we set off for the longer ride across the East River by one of the bridges in the north of Manhattan, then through the borough of Queens, and finally out into the bleak countryside of Long Island. It was like entering another world—a land of snow and silence.

"Where are we going?" Emmy asked nervously. "Are we going back to England?"

"You need a boat for that, silly," Tig said.

"We are going to meet your grandfather," Miss Van Woekem said. "Make sure you are on your best behavior."

"Will our mummy be there?" Emmy asked.

I glanced at Miss Van Woekem, both of us unsure how to answer this.

"I'm afraid not," I said.

We were cold, stiff, and tired from the jolting by the time we entered the gates and arrived at Fairview. Julia had spotted the carriage and came out to meet us.

"Aunt Olivia, what a lovely surprise," she said, her face alight with joy. "So you changed your mind and decided to join us for Christmas after all?"

"I have come on a mission," the old lady said as she was helped down from the carriage. "I have brought these children to see their grandfather."

"Their grandfather?" Julia looked confused.

"They are Margaret Montague's children, recently arrived from England," Miss Van Woekem said. "And this is my dear friend, Mrs. Sullivan, who was gracious enough to accompany me."

Julia looked at me, puzzled, then gave a tinkling laugh. "So you were here on a secret mission when last we met. You brought the present from Godmother, didn't you?"

I smiled and didn't deny it.

We stepped into the delightful warmth of the house. There was now an enormous Christmas tree in the foyer and the children gazed at it in wonder. Servants helped us off with coats and hats. If one of them recognized me from my previous visit, they were too well trained to say so.

"First you must have a hot drink," Julia said. "Your hands are freezing. Pratchett, tell cook to make us all hot chocolate. And bring some cookies for the children."

She led us through to the morning room, where a huge fire blazed in the hearth. I perched on the edge of my chair, so tense I felt I might snap at any moment. Miss Van Woekem seemed so confident, but she had not seen how wily and dangerous Eustace Everett could be. The hot chocolate had just arrived when we heard the clatter of boots down the tiled hall and Eustace himself came in.

He looked at us with surprise. "Aunt Olivia, what a pleasant surprise," he said, then frowned as he turned his gaze to myself and the children.

"I have brought some friends with me," Miss Van Woekem said. "I believe you have met Mrs. Sullivan, but not your young cousins. This is Thomas and this is Megan. Your cousin Margaret's children, who have come to see their grandfather."

Eustace's face flushed beet red. "What absolute nonsense is this?" He turned on me. "This is your doing, isn't it?" he bellowed. Then he swung back to her. "You stupid old woman—you've allowed yourself to be fooled by a confidence trickster. These are not my cousin's children. They are urchins she's dragged from the streets."

"And if I have been given proof of their identity?" Miss Van Woekem asked calmly.

"There is no proof of that at all. Margaret Montague ran off to England years ago and hasn't been heard from since. No proof she ever came back to America."

"Ah, but there is," I said.

"What proof?" he shouted.

"I plan to show that to her father," I said. "Now if you

will stand aside, we are going to take the children up to see him."

"You're certainly not going up there." Eustace gave a menacing step toward me. "In fact you'd better leave now, before I summon the police."

"Eustace!" Julia exclaimed. "That's no way to talk to my godmother's friend."

"I take it that Mr. Montague is still alive?" I asked.

"He is, but while he is incapacitated I am master of this house and I absolutely forbid it. Now you will please leave if you know what is good for you." Eustace was glaring at me with hatred in his eyes.

"I think it would be up to Mr. Montague to make up his mind whether these are his grandchildren or not," I said.

Eustace was still standing blocking the doorway. "He is not up to visitors. In fact he is close to death—he may not even make it to Christmas."

"All the more reason that he should make his peace with his grandchildren now," Miss Van Woekem said. "Come, children. Take my hands."

And she walked toward the door. Eustace stood there, uncertain how to react. Obviously he didn't want to stop his fiancée's godmother by force.

"What makes you think he will even want to see those children?" he demanded. "He told Margaret she was no longer his daughter when she ran off with that Welsh peasant. He hasn't even mentioned her name ever since. She is dead to him."

"We'll have to see, won't we?" Miss Van Woekem said

evenly. "If he doesn't want to acknowledge them, so be it." She turned to a footman who was standing in the doorway. "Please escort us to Mr. Montague's room."

The footman shot a frightened glance at Eustace.

"I'll show you," Julia said. "Come on, my precious." And she took Emmy's hand.

As I passed Eustace I drew him aside. "I have but one word to say to you, Mr. Everett," I said. "Stallion." And I gave him a knowing nod.

I was delighted by the instant reaction this produced as I followed the others up the stairs. I could sense him standing there, watching me, probably trying to decide what to do next. Mr. Montague was still on the third floor in a room off that Spartan hallway. Julia and I arrived before Miss Van Woekem, who was taking the two flights of stairs slowly. Mr. Montague's door was half open and I heard a female voice saying, "Time for your hot milk, Mr. Montague. Let me help you to sit up."

I surged ahead of the others and snatched the milk away as the nurse was putting it to his lips. "Don't drink it, Mr. Montague," I said. "You're being drugged."

"What are you doing? Who do you think you are?" the nurse demanded as I wrestled the cup away. Hot liquid spilled across the bed and floor. The nurse gave a cry of anger, grabbed a towel, and tried to mop it up. "Now look what you've done. Are you out of your mind?"

The old man looked up, trying to focus on me. "Who are you?"

"Someone who cares enough to save you," I said. "And I've brought some special people to see you."

Julia had entered the room with Tig and Emmy. She pushed them forward as I beckoned. The old man sat up and rubbed his eyes.

"Meggie?" he said in a quavering voice. "Is that my Meggie come back to me? It can't be. She's gone. I'm so confused." He passed a hand over his face.

"Not your daughter, Mr. Montague, but your grandchild. Margaret's children," I said. "This is Thomas and this is Megan."

A frown crossed his face. "My daughter is gone. She has not been in touch with me once in almost ten years. You're trying to tell me she's come back home?"

"I'm afraid your daughter is dead, Mr. Montague," I said, and heard a gasp from the children. I realized instantly I should have handled this better and broken the news to them gently at an appropriate time.

"Mummy is dead?" Emmy asked, turning big eyes toward me.

"I thought so," Tig said solemnly. "Otherwise she'd never have left us in that horrible place."

"How do you know my daughter is dead?" Mr. Montague demanded, now sitting up and more alert.

I really didn't want to go on with this in front of the children. Knowing their mother was dead was bad enough, but hearing that she was murdered was something no child should ever hear. But I also had this one chance to convince their grandfather that they belonged to him.

"Tig, you two go and look out of the window and see if it's snowing again," I said. He glanced at me as if he understood and took Emmy's hand. When they were sufficiently far away, I opened my purse. "I have a picture of her." I handed it to him.

He took the photograph in trembling hands and nodded. "Yes, this is my daughter. But where was it taken?"

"Her body was photographed at the morgue after she was found in the East River. I'm afraid she was murdered."

"My daughter was murdered?" He took a moment to collect himself then looked up at me. "If she had come back to America, why didn't she come home? Why didn't she try to contact me?"

"She wrote to you, at least once," I said. "But Mrs. Braithwaite said that she saw your nephew intercept the letter. She recognized the handwriting and was about to take it up to you when your nephew took it and stuffed it into his pocket."

"Where is Mrs. Braithwaite?" Mr. Montague looked around, bewildered. "I haven't seen her lately."

"Eustace dismissed her immediately after that incident. Who knows how many letters he had prevented you from seeing?"

"Eustace did this? Where is he?" Mr. Montague demanded. "What does he have to say for himself?"

"I'll go and find him," Julia said. "I'm sure Eustace couldn't have done these horrible things. There must be an explanation."

Mr. Montague, his face as thin, drawn, and gray as a skeleton's, lay propped against his pillows, studying the children.

Eustace himself came into the room. "I tried to stop them from bothering you, Uncle. I know how sick you are, but these women insisted on your seeing these children. But I have to tell you there is no proof at all that they are Margaret's children. From what I've discovered they were begging on the street until this woman rescued them for her own devices. No doubt she hopes to make money out of this."

"Fiddlesticks," Miss Van Woekem said, coming closer to Mr. Montague. "I have known Mrs. Sullivan for years and I can attest that she is as straight as a die. And what's more, her husband is a distinguished member of the New York police department, as was his father before him."

"And if you want proof, Mr. Montague, you can ask the children to describe an item of jewelry their mother always wore," I said.

I glanced across at Tig, who had been staring in wide-eyed fear. He stepped forward. "She wore a locket all the time. She never took it off."

"That's right." Mr. Montague nodded. "Her mother wore it until she died and after her death Margaret started to wear it, to remember her mother by. What did this locket look like?"

Tig smiled at the memory. "It had pearls all around the edge and her initials on it and inside there were two locks of hair, and they look like Emmy's but Mummy said that one was hers and one was her brother's."

Mr. Montague was now staring at them in wonder. "Quite right," he said.

"The children had that locket in their possession until it was taken away by trickery—by your nephew," I said, not looking at Eustace. "And I gather that your daughter had a lovely singing voice. Emmy also has a beautiful voice. Can you sing one of your mother's songs for your grandfather?"

Emmy looked up at me. I put an arm around her shoulder, and she started to sing.

Golden slumbers kiss your eyes,
Smiles awake you when you rise,
Sleep, little darling, do not cry,
And I will sing a lullaby.

She looked up at her grandfather. "That was a song Mummy always sang me at bedtime."

The old man now had tears streaming down his face. "That was one of Margaret's favorite songs," he said. "My wife always sang it to her at bedtime too. And this little lady looks just like her." He held out his hands to Emmy. "Come, child. Give your old grandfather a kiss before he dies."

"You're not going to die, Mr. Montague. I think we're in time to save you. I suspect you've been drugged for some time now . . . maybe poisoned as well," I said.

"What is that?" He looked across at the nurse, who was now standing in the doorway. "What have you been giving me?"

"Only what your doctor prescribed, Mr. Montague. Nothing else."

"I saw her putting a spoonful of a white powder into your hot milk, Mr. Montague," I said.

"Of course. That was the medicine he'd been prescribed to calm his stomach. I just did what I was directed," the nurse said.

"That powder is now with the police, being analyzed," I said. "If there's nothing wrong with it, then you've nothing to worry about."

"I'm only the nurse. I do as I'm told," she said, "and Mr. Everett gave me the tin with the directions printed on it."

"Maybe Mr. Everett can give us the name and address of the doctor who prescribed the medicine?" I turned to look at Eustace but he wasn't there.

"Eustace?" Julia called. "Eustace, come back and explain yourself. Tell them you did nothing wrong."

Eustace came back into the room. He pushed past me and went right up to his uncle. "This stops right now," he said. "I have worked hard all these years to make sure your business prospers in your absence, Uncle. I have earned my inheritance and I refuse to be cheated out of it by a couple of street brats, by the spawn of a nobody from the gutter."

"My father wasn't a nobody!" Tig said angrily, bravely stepping up to face Eustace. "He took good care of us. And my mummy loved him."

"Please spare me the sentiment," Eustace said. "And don't think of changing your will, Uncle. If you do, I'll take you to court and prove that you are of unsound mind. Do you think the courts will acknowledge the children as his legal heirs with no documents and no proof?"

"But you'll have to do without my money, Eustace," Julia said. "How could I have been so blind? I thought you were a nice person but I can't believe how badly you're treating your relatives. I can't marry such a man. Aunt Olivia, do you have your carriage? I want to go home, please."

"No, Julia, you don't understand," Eustace said. He tried to grab her arm. She shook him off. "It's these people. They have twisted the truth."

"As to that, Mr. Everett, it is you who has twisted the truth," I said. "What about your cousin's locket that you stole? And the letters your uncle never received from his daughter? And do you think that Julia will still want to marry you when she learns of the company you keep and the clubs you frequent?"

Eustace's face flushed angrily again. He turned on me, raising a menacing hand, and for a second I thought he was going to strike me. "You meddlesome bitch," he said. "I'll make you pay for this."

"Enough, Eustace," Mr. Montague said in a voice stronger than I would have believed possible. "Get out of my house. I never want to see you again."

"I'll go," Eustace said, suddenly icily calm, "but if I do, then they go with me." And to my horror he produced a pistol from his pocket. He pointed it at the children. "You two. Over here. Now." He grabbed Emmy by the hair, dragging her to his side, then held the gun at her head. She let out a little whimper. Other than that the room had gone silent.

"Come on, march. We're going for a ride." He waved the gun around at the rest of us, who stood frozen as if in some horrible tableau. "And if you try to stop me, I won't hesitate to kill them. In fact it will give me considerable pleasure."

We watched helplessly as he forced the children down the stairs. Then we saw them put into the backseat of his automobile, Emmy's little face staring up at the house as if begging us to rescue her. Eustace cranked the automobile and it roared to life. I couldn't wait a second longer. I ran down the stairs, followed by Julia and her godmother, and we watched from the doorway as the car disappeared down the drive. It was now snowing hard, great white flakes falling silently to blot out the world.

"Your carriage, quickly," I shouted. It was still standing there, the horses under a snow-covered blanket and the driver standing beside it, wrapped in a rug and looking miserable. Julia and I piled inside the carriage and we took off at a canter. The carriage swayed as we turned onto the narrow lane and plowed through the new snow. We clung on. It was hard going for the horses. The snow fell faster and faster until it was swirling around us in a world of whiteness.

"We can't go on like this," the coachman called down. "I can't see two yards in front of me. That automobile will be long gone."

"He's right," Julia said. "We should go back and call the police."

"By then the children will be dead," I said. "Please just try and make it into Great Neck. It can't be far now."

We came around a sharp bend and the carriage jerked suddenly to a halt. One of the horses let out a frightened neigh. I let down the window and leaned out, as snow swirled into my face.

The driver had climbed down. The horses were stamping nervously. Through the blizzard there was a hissing noise. "Don't look, ma'am," he said.

I ignored this remark and let myself out of the carriage. The automobile had skidded off the road at the bend and had hit a tree. Its front was buckled in and Eustace Everett lay sprawled across the steering wheel, unconscious or dead. Frankly I didn't care which at the moment.

"Where are the children?" I shouted, and pushed past the coachman. The backseat of the car was empty. A lump came into my throat. He had killed them already and dumped their bodies. But surely he had not had enough time to do that . . . I looked around and picked up a small footprint and then signs that someone had scrambled up a snowbank beside the road. They had survived and fled while they could. But a blizzard was now blowing and they were not wearing any outer garments. Neither was I for that matter.

"Julia," I shouted. "Go on into Great Neck and get help. Tell them the children are lost in the storm. I'm going to try and find them."

"But you've no coat on," she said.

"Neither have they. I must find them before it's too late," I said.

"Here, take this." She threw me down the traveling rug that was in the carriage. I draped it around my head and shoulders as the carriage disappeared into the gloom. I heard the jingle of harness long after I could see them. I slithered up the bank and tried to spot another small footprint. It was snowing so hard that I'd have to work quickly before they were all covered. But then I spotted one. It was facing in the direction of a stand of trees on the other side of the field. Snow blinded me as I slithered and stumbled forward, sometimes plunging into snow up to my knees. I could no longer see more than a foot in front of me, and I plowed on guided only by instinct and desperation. I don't know how long I blundered in that nightmare. I could no longer feel my feet or hands. My face stung. My eyes watered and my breathing was ragged. I realized how stupid I had been to have attempted this. Now quite possibly I'd die in the snow as well as the children. I thought of Liam and Daniel and Bridie. How could I have let them down like this?

Surely there must be some kind of homestead somewhere out here, I thought. What about all those mansions we had passed? And the market gardens and small holdings. People live out here. It's not that far from New York City. And as soon as I'd bucked myself up with those thoughts I saw a dark shape through the blizzard. It formed itself into a small hut or shed. I stumbled up to it and lifted the latch on the door. The warm herby smell of cow dung greeted me and I saw two cows looking at me anxiously. I took off the snow-covered rug and shook off the coating of snow. As I did so I heard a sound—a gasp, and there in one corner were the children, huddled together.

"It's all right," I said. "I'm here. That man won't be coming after you anymore."

And they rushed into my arms.

"We'll have to stay here until the storm dies down," I said. "But the cows will help keep us warm."

I found enough clean straw and we huddled together under the rug. I don't know how long we were there. I think we might all have drifted off to sleep. Then through my half-consciousness I heard a sound—the sweet ringing of a distant bell. And suddenly it came to me. It was Christmas Eve and those were the first bells of Christmas. We really were away in a manger and we were going to be safe.

❧ Twenty-six ❧

I t was later that day when a big cart horse pulling a sleigh finally found us. We were bundled in rugs and taken into Great Neck. There we learned from the local sheriff that Eustace Everett had been taken to hospital and was expected to recover. The sheriff was pleased about that, as Eustace would now have to face kidnapping and attempted murder charges. I found out that the sheriff had received a wire, presumably from Daniel, giving him the result of the chemical analysis. The mixture given to Mr. Montague had contained arsenic, opium, and barbiturate. So I had been right. Mr. Montague was being drugged and poisoned.

We were taken back out to the estate and received warmly by a very worried Mr. Montague and Miss Van Woekem. After a good hot meal it was decided that the children should return to Sid and Gus for the time being, until their grandfather was recovered to good health. I was glad about that as I knew Sid and Gus were looking forward to celebrating Christmas with them and had surely bought far too many presents. Emmy sat on my lap and Tig snuggled against me as we undertook the long carriage ride back to the city. Fortunately the snow had abated, but it was still hard going and the journey seemed to take forever. Julia and Miss Van Woekem sat facing us. Julia stared out of the window, saying nothing. I thought she was being very brave. To have found out the man she planned to marry had such an evil side must have been a horrible shock to her.

It was only when the carriage stopped at the entrance to Patchin Place that she said, "I have to thank you, Mrs. Sullivan. You saved me from a life of grief. Eustace promised me the moon—trips to Europe, and of course to be mistress of Fairview. It all seemed so exciting."

"I don't think you'd have enjoyed being mistress of Fairview for long," I said. "I am rather afraid you might have met the same fate as Margaret and her brother and father."

"Don't." She shuddered. "How can any man be such a monster?"

"There is both good and evil in the world," Miss Van Woekem said. "But you and I shall celebrate Christmas together, Julia."

"You'd be very welcome to join us for Christmas dinner tomorrow," I said. I'd said it more out of politeness, but I saw a pleased expression on Miss Van Woekem's face.

"Really? How kind. I can think of nothing better than Christmas with a family. That is how it should be celebrated."

Relief flooded Daniel's face when he saw us. "You're safe. Thank God. I was so worried. When that man came to the door, telling me what the mixture contained, I was afraid for you. It felt terrible being stuck here and able to do nothing. I sent a cable but got no reply."

"We were delayed by the snowstorm," I said, smiling as I kissed his forehead. "Mr. Everett tried to escape but his automobile hit a tree. So he is in hospital and will be arrested for attempted murder."

"And Mr. Montague? Will he survive, do you think?"

"I think he will make a splendid recovery with no more drugs in his system. He'll need building up, of course, but Mrs. Braithwaite will see to that."

"And will he welcome his grandchildren?" he asked.

"Absolutely. Although it will be hard for Sid and Gus to give them up."

"Nonsense," Daniel said with a laugh. "In a few weeks they'll be planning a trip to Outer Mongolia or learning to fly an aeroplane."

When darkness fell we lit the candles on the Christmas tree and roasted chestnuts on the fire. I sat with my son on my lap, contentedly sucking his thumb while he gazed in wonder at the flickering candlelight on the tree. Bridie snuggled up beside me and I smiled to my husband across the fire, thinking what a lucky person I was to be safe and warm and spending Christmas with my family.

Bells awoke us, ringing out glad tidings all over the city. We all went to early mass, even Daniel managed to walk that far, his arm tucked through mine. Then stockings were discovered by the fireplace. Liam's dog was too big to fit in a stocking but he gave a delighted squeal when Daniel wheeled it in to him. Bridie took the nuts, the orange, and the sugar mouse out of her stocking, thanking us politely. Then her eyes grew wide as she unwrapped the doll from its festive paper. For a moment I thought she was going to cry.

"It's the most beautiful doll I have ever seen," she stammered.

"A doll? At your age?" Daniel's mother said, frowning. "Aren't you a little old for it?"

"Bridie can learn to sew by making outfits for it," I said, trying to swallow back anger that she had spoiled Bridie's moment.

She had nothing negative to say about the book on Ireland, however. Daniel was delighted with his whiskey and his tobacco jar, and then he handed me a small package. In it was a delicate blue enamel watch on a pin shaped like a bow.

"Daniel. It's lovely," I stammered.

"I thought that you, more than anybody, needed to know how to keep track of time," he said. He pinned it on my front. I glanced at myself in the looking glass—me, Molly Murphy, actually owning a watch of her own!

The turkey was stuffed and put in the oven. The rest of the meal was prepared when Sid, Gus, and the children came over to join us. Of course there were more gifts and much excitement. Sid and Gus were delighted with their book on Indian cooking.

"How fortuitous, Molly," Gus said. "We were just saying it was time we went to India. Sid is determined to ride an elephant, you see."

Daniel caught my eye and he winked.

At around noon Miss Van Woekem and Julia arrived. Sherry was drunk and at two o'clock the turkey was carved and served. After we were full of turkey and puddings and pies, we retired to the parlor, where we played charades and word games until it was time to light the candles again on the tree. Then we sat around, singing carols. As I listened to Emmy's sweet voice I thought about that first time we had heard her, huddled in her doorway. I hoped her parents were looking down on her now, glad that she was finally safe and happy.